## "You wanna spend time with me?"

His devastatingly handsome smile returned. "I'd like the opportunity. Why is it you seem so surprised by that?"

"Because…" Had a man ever taken the time to get to know her? What if Nathan found her lacking as other men had? The thought he might be disappointed in what he discovered had her faltering with her response.

"Alyssa…" he prodded gently.

She sighed deeply. "Because I'm not perfect."

"And you think I am?" he replied with a husky chuckle. "Far from," he admitted. "Just ask my brothers."

"It's not that simple," she said.

"Nothing in life is simple," he told her. "I've learned that the hard way. When my wife died, I forgot how to breathe. How to feel. I put on a brave face for my daughter, but inside I was filled with a never-ending numbness." He glanced her way. "And then you came into our life. I can't explain it, but when I'm around you I feel like I can breathe again."

**Kat Brookes** is an award-winning author and past Romance Writers of America Golden Heart® Award finalist. She is married to her childhood sweetheart and has been blessed with two beautiful daughters. She loves writing stories that can both make you smile and touch your heart. Kat is represented by Michelle Grajkowski with 3 Seas Literary Agency. Read more about Kat and her upcoming releases at katbrookes.com. Email her at katbrookes@comcast.net. Facebook: Kat Brookes.

## Books by Kat Brookes

### Love Inspired

#### *Texas Sweethearts*

*Her Texas Hero*
*His Holiday Matchmaker*

# His Holiday
# Matchmaker

## Kat Brookes

HARLEQUIN® LOVE INSPIRED®

LOVE INSPIRED BOOKS

ISBN-13: 978-0-373-81947-8

His Holiday Matchmaker

Copyright © 2016 by Kimberly Duffy

**Printed in U.S.A.**

And God is able to bless you abundantly, so that in all things at all times, having all that you need, you will abound in every good work.
—*2 Corinthians* 9:8

In memory of my mother-in-law, who went home to the Lord this past Christmas. You were more than a mother-in-law to me. You were my second mother. I thank you for giving me the wonderful man I am married to. You will be missed more than you could ever know.

# Chapter One

"Daddy! Daddy!"

"Cupcake!" Nathan Cooper replied with a grin as he swung his six-year-old daughter, Katie, up into the air.

She burst into a fit of girlish giggles. "I'm not a cupcake."

"Sure you are," he said as he lowered her to the ground. Reaching out, he ruffled her unruly curls. "Look at all this chocolate frosting."

"That's my hair," she said with another giggle, flashing him a smile that reminded him so much of her mother it hurt. So much of Isabel lived on in their daughter. Her dark eyes. Those long brown curls. That determined chin.

Nathan tamped down the memories of his late wife that threatened to surface. Forcing his focus solely on the tiny heart-shaped face looking up at him so adoringly, he playfully pinched his daughter's lightly freckled cheek. "And I suppose these aren't sprinkles?"

"No, silly. They're freckles!" She pulled away with another giggle and ran back to the porch. "Watch what I can do, Daddy."

He smiled as she dipped a large bubble wand into the bright yellow tray that sat on the sun-warmed porch steps and then spun in a slow circle, her motion creating a long, iridescent bubble. *To be so carefree*, he thought with an inner sigh.

The door to the small, ranch-style house creaked open, drawing his gaze that way.

"Nathan," Mildred Timmons greeted with a warm smile. A smiling, robust woman in her midsixties, Mildred had been a Godsend to him after losing both his wife and his parents in the storm two years before.

He'd been a couple of towns away, working on a construction project with his brothers, when the F4 tornado touched down, leaving a path of destruction across several Texas counties. The near mile-wide twister had swept across the northernmost part of Braxton, ripping down power lines, damaging buildings and taking the lives of those he loved in a few short minutes.

"You're done early," she said, wiping her hands on the apron she had tied about her rounded waist.

"Not really. I have a break before I have to get back to the site. Thought I'd take Katie into town for a hot dog. That is, unless she's already eaten dinner."

"You're in luck. She hasn't. We were gonna make some fish sticks and fries, but I'm sure she'd rather be having dinner with her daddy. You two haven't gotten to share many meals together lately."

He nodded with a frown. As co-owner of Cooper Construction, a business he'd started with his brother Carter five years earlier, he'd had his hands full dealing with the reconstruction needs left behind in the area by the tornado that struck two Decembers ago.

"We're working overtime to get the recreation center finished before Christmas Eve, but a few unexpected setbacks are pushing us down to the wire." With so many people counting on him and his brothers to get the job done in time, the pressure was on. He couldn't let the town down. Couldn't let Isabel down. Not only did the town council plan to hold their annual community holiday festivities in the newly erected building, they had decided to dedicate the new rec center to the townsfolk that were lost in the storm. So while he hadn't been there for Isabel when she'd needed him most, he was determined to do whatever it took to see to it the dedication took place as planned. That her memory lived on.

"I have faith in you boys," Millie said. "You'll make it in time."

*Faith*—it was something he used to hold dear to his heart. That was before he'd lost those he loved in a violent, senseless storm.

"Just don't stretch yourself too thin," she warned, drawing Nathan from his troubled thoughts. "Katie needs you."

And he needed her, too. But it was during this particular time of year he needed to bury himself in his work. Needed to forget about the future that had been so unfairly taken from him. From Katie.

"I might be a little late tonight," he said, avoiding the issue of his demanding work schedule. "Will that be a problem?"

"Oh, goodness, no," the older woman replied as her gaze followed the energetic six-year-old around the yard. "I love having Katie here with me. She's such a breath of fresh air for an old woman like me."

"You're far from old," he told her.

"Old enough," Millie countered.

"You know, Millie, I don't know what we would've done without you these past two years."

"I could say the same thing about all of you,"

she said, her voice catching. Her husband had been the only other tornado-related fatality in Braxton. He'd been out doing a check of the property's fence line when the storm struck and he hadn't been able to make it to shelter. "You boys, little Katie here, and Carter's lovely wife and children have become my family. I just wish…" She looked his way, her expression doleful.

"Wish what?"

"That you would open yourself up to love again."

He sighed. "Millie…"

"I know we've discussed this before," she admitted. "But I can't help it. I wanna see you meet a nice young lady like Carter did. Be happy again. You're too young to spend the rest of your life alone."

His brother was happy. No doubt about it. Audra and her two young children meant the world to Carter. But what if something happened to that perfect world he'd walked so willingly into? Like it had to his and Isabel's?

"I'm not alone," he said, fighting a frown. "I have Katie." Though he'd nearly lost her, too, when his own perfect world came crashing down around him. Isabel had taken their young daughter out to his parents' ranch to help put up their Christmas tree when the twister struck.

Katie and his father had been pulled from the rubble and taken to the hospital. Katie survived. His father hadn't, dying a day after his beloved wife and daughter-in-law.

"Have faith," his father had said during his final moments in the hospital. "There is always hope beyond the storm."

But was there really?

"Yes, you do," Millie agreed with an empathetic smile. "All the more reason for you to start living again. Besides, Katie needs a woman in her life."

"She already does. Two, in fact. She has you and Audra." Turning, he whistled to get his daughter's attention. "Park your bubble wand, Cupcake. Daddy's taking you to Big Dog's for dinner."

"Big Dog's!" she squealed in delight. "Yay!"

He turned back to Mildred. "Would you like to join us?"

"Thank you for the offer, but I have a hankering for fish sticks for dinner," she told him with a kind smile. "You go spend some special time with your little girl."

He nodded. "We'll be back in an hour or so." That said, he stepped from the porch. Scooping up his daughter, he carried the giggling little girl out to his truck.

He and Katie were fine just the way they were.

\* \* \*

"Well, if it isn't my two favorite customers."

"Hey, Lizzie!" Katie said with a toothy grin.

"Hey, Katie," the young waitress replied. "I see you roped your daddy into taking you out for dinner again."

"She's pretty good at wrangling me into doing her bidding," Nathan admitted with a chuckle. Lizzie was a sweetheart who was loved by all. She had been waitressing at Big Dog's ever since graduating from high school. "How's school going?"

"It's going," she said. "A little challenging juggling work and my online classes, but I'm determined to get that degree before I'm too old to do anything with it."

"You're only twenty-four," he reminded her.

"Sometimes it feels like I'm twice that."

"You'll manage," he assured her with a nod.

"I wish I could be as certain as you are," she replied. "It won't be long before I'm working, taking online classes and squeezing in the required classes that have to be taken at school. My head is bound to be spinning soon."

"Keep your eye on the goal," he told her. "That meteorology degree you're working toward will help save lives down the road."

The worry left her face, replaced by a bright smile. "Thanks for the pep talk. Why don't you go grab yourselves a table while I fetch a couple of menus?"

He looked to his daughter. "Where are we sitting today, Cupcake?" His daughter liked to pick a different one each time they came in.

"Over here," she exclaimed, skipping to an empty table halfway across the room.

He followed, sitting on one of the chairs with its bright red padded vinyl seat. The bell over the restaurant's front door jingled, drawing Nathan's gaze in that direction. Two young women he'd never seen before stepped inside. Both looked to be in their midtwenties. The first had straight, dark hair that stopped at her shoulders. The one walking in behind her had long, red-gold hair that shimmered like flames under the fluorescent lighting of the diner as she moved toward him.

He tipped his cowboy hat with a polite nod as they walked by. "Ladies." Then he removed it, placing it on the seat of the empty chair beside him.

Both offered up warm smiles, but where the first woman remained focused on finding a table, the fiery-haired woman slowed, her topaz gaze lingering in his direction for a long moment before she continued on to where her friend had slid into an empty booth.

The way the woman had studied him had

Nathan wondering if they hadn't crossed paths somewhere before. Surely, he would have remembered a face like hers if he had. Especially, those eyes. He'd never seen any quite that color. Like warmed honey with flecks of gold mixed in.

Lizzie returned with their menus and two glasses of ice water. "I'll give you a couple of minutes to look the menu over."

"Appreciate it," he told her, opening one of the menus as she walked away. Try as he might, Nathan couldn't keep his gaze from sliding over to the booth the two women were seated in. The one with the darker hair sat with her back to his and Katie's table. The other, the one whose searching gaze had come to rest on him for the briefest of moments, faced his way. Her attention, however, was now focused solely on her friend and the conversation they had immediately fallen into, giving him plenty of opportunity to study her more closely.

Delicate features made up her face with the exception of her boldly lashed amber eyes. Bow-shaped lips pursed together as she cast a glance out the window beside her. A second later, perfectly straight, white teeth were sinking into her bottom lip as if she were deeply troubled by something.

It was none of his business, but Nathan found himself wondering what she was worried about.

"Daddy," his daughter whined from across the table, drawing his attention back to the task at hand.

"Have you decided?" he asked her with a smile.

"Strawberry! Strawberry! Strawberry!"

Nathan chuckled as his daughter bounced up and down on the padded booth seat, excitement lighting her face. "I thought chocolate was your favorite milk shake flavor."

She stopped bouncing and looked up at him from across the table. "Daddy, it's a girl's peroggertiv to change her mind."

His eyes widened at the unexpected response. "Prerogative?"

Katie rolled her eyes. "That's what I said."

"So you did," he chuckled. "You know, that's a mighty big word for a six-year-old."

"Almost seven," she reminded him. "And Granny Timmons says it every time she breaks her one-cookie-before-supper rule and gives me another one."

Nathan couldn't help but smile. Suddenly, Lizzie hurried back to the table. "Sorry to keep you waiting. I had to handle a carryout order." She flipped open the order pad in her hand and poised her pen over it. "What can I get for the two of you?"

Dragging his focus back to the menu, he said, "Hmm...let's see. We'll take three super dogs, ketchup on one, mustard on the other two, a large order of fries and a strawberry milk shake."

"Will that be all?"

He cast a glance at his daughter over the top of his menu. "How about we make that *two* strawberry shakes? But we'd like those *after* my little Cupcake here eats all her dinner."

"You've got it, Mr. Cooper." Shoving her pencil behind her ear, Lizzie went to place their order.

"Daddy, do you got to go back to work?" his daughter asked, her tiny lips forming a soft pout.

He nodded. "For a little while, honey."

Her small shoulders sagged at his response.

Guilt tugged at him. "Tell you what. I'll see what I can do about taking the whole weekend off so you and I can do something special. How's that sound?"

Her face lit up. "Can we go Christmas shopping?"

An all-too-familiar twinge moved through his heart. One that came every year during the holidays. He didn't want to shop for presents or put up endless strings of Christmas lights to make his house festive. If it were up to him, he'd by-pass the season altogether. But he couldn't do that to Katie.

"How about we take a walk over to The Toy Box after dinner and start putting together your wish list? Then maybe we can see a movie this weekend."

"I already know what I want," she replied with a toothy smile.

He leaned forward, arms folded atop the table in front of him. "Let me guess. You want a new swing set?"

She shook her head, sending her head full of dark brown curls bouncing. "Nope."

"A doll?"

"Uncle Logan just bought me a new dolly. Guess again," his daughter urged with youthful impatience.

Rubbing his chin as if in deep thought, he hemmed and hawed for several seconds before saying, "I know. You want a giant pink pony?"

Katie giggled. "That's silly, Daddy."

"Okay, I give up. What do you really want for Christmas?"

She leaned forward, folding her arms just like his were and said determinedly, "I want a mommy."

Nathan was speechless. She'd had a mommy. And he'd had a wife. How could he make Katie understand that no other woman could ever fill the void left behind when Isabel died?

"You have your daddy," he pointed out, trying to sound unaffected by the turn in their conversation, when in truth he was anything but.

"I know, but Bettina's mommy braids her hair every morning before school."

"I can braid your hair." He'd done so for three of the birthday parties Katie had been invited to that past year and had done a pretty good job of it if he did say so himself.

"But her mommy makes a French braid."

He hated feeling like he had somehow failed his daughter. Something he never wanted to do. "I'll see what I can do."

Her eyes lit up. "About getting me a mommy?"

"About learning how to French braid your hair."

She sank back against the padded seat, crossing her tiny arms. "But I want a mommy."

"That's not gonna happen, Cupcake," he told her, fighting to keep the turmoil going on inside him from his voice.

Her stubbornness kicking in, his daughter lifted her chin and pouted.

"Katie," he began, only to be saved from saying anything else as Lizzie came back with their orders, instantly distracting his daughter from her mommy quest. Thankfully. Marrying again was not an option for him.

And it never would be.

December first had finally arrived. Alyssa McCall walked her best friend back to her SUV, a tight ball of anxiety in her stomach.

"Are you sure you wanna do this?" Erica asked.

She nodded. "Yes." Despite her fears and reservations, Alyssa truly felt that this was where she needed to be. Where the Lord wanted her to be. Not only would she be helping to reconstruct a part of the town that had been destroyed by the tornado, she would be proving herself to the interior design firm she worked for.

Since the car accident that had nearly taken her life three years before, she'd gone from being a highly sought after interior designer working full-time to being placed on the back burner with her firm, only being given small, mostly part-time jobs.

Pure Perfection Designs, the firm she'd been working for since college, felt that her visual disability, damage done specifically to the visual cortex of her brain in the accident that left her medically diagnosed as "legally blind," left her incapable of handling the more intricate design planning and extensive hands-on attention their customers were seeking. While the pathway sending visual messages from her eyes to her brain didn't always function as it should, she could still manage to perform the tasks required of her job. So this opportunity in Braxton was her chance to prove herself. To her firm and to herself.

"Isn't there some other way you can contribute to the cause without having to stay so long?" Erica asked with a frown as they stopped beside her friend's shiny new silver Ford Explorer. "We're talking about spending most of December in a town where you don't know anyone."

Alyssa laughed softly. "Hey! Weren't you the one giving me the you-can-do-this pep talk back at Big Dog's when I went into that teeny tiny panic attack?"

"Sorry," her friend apologized. "I have all the faith in the world you can do this. Really I do. It's just the mom in me coming out. It can't be helped."

"It's okay," Alyssa said with a grateful smile. "It's nice to know I have someone in my life that truly cares about me."

"The right man is gonna come along," her friend assured her, knowing that Alyssa longed to have the kind of family Erica had.

"Not if I keep dating Mr. Not-So-Rights." Not that she had dated much since the accident.

As soon as her dates found out she was legally blind, they bailed. She supposed she couldn't blame them. A relationship with her would involve some major adjustments. But at least her visual impairment wouldn't get any worse than it was now. She could live with that, even if the men she had dated couldn't.

"Don't give up on love," Erica beseeched her. "Mr. Right is out there."

Reaching out, Alyssa opened the back passenger door to collect her suitcase. "I suppose I'll just have to take your word for it."

She leaned into the vehicle and grabbed her suitcase. Lowering the black spinner onto the sidewalk beside her, she stepped away from the SUV and turned to her friend. "I guess I'll see you in a few weeks. Maybe sooner."

Erica gave her a hug. "If you change your mind about doing this—"

"I know," she said, cutting her off with a grin. "You're only a phone call away."

"I'll miss you," Erica called out as she made her way around to the driver's side door.

"Same here," she replied, lifting her hand in a wave as her friend drove away. Then she stood watching as the blurred image of her friend's SUV disappeared from sight. A sudden surge of panic had her entire body tensing.

Her hand moved over the soft leather of the

purse she had draped across her as she fought the urge to dig inside it for her cell phone. No, she thought determinedly, she would not call Erica to come back for her. Fear would not control her. She could do this. Closing her eyes, she prayed for the Lord to give her the strength to do what she had come to do. As she did so, a sense of calm slowly settled over her.

Opening her eyes, she let her gaze drift down what she knew to be the main street of town. Braxton, much smaller than San Antonio according to the information she'd found on the town's website, stretched out before her in a distortion of shapes and colors. The closer buildings she could almost make out, just not the fine details. Never since the damage done to her vision from the accident had she felt the loss of her perfect eyesight more. She was far from familiar surroundings in a town where she knew no one. At the same time, she was grateful that her impaired vision would get no worse when so many others were forced to live their lives in total darkness.

"Hurry up, Daddy!" a tiny voice squealed behind her.

Alyssa turned just as a flash of red whooshed by, bumping into her with enough force to knock her off-balance.

"Sorry!" the little girl called back over her shoulder as she raced away.

A strong hand closed around Alyssa's arm to steady her. "Sorry about that," a deep, very male voice apologized. "I'm afraid my daughter had a little too much sugar at dinner."

Her gaze climbed up the giant of a man standing before her. He had broad shoulders, a black cowboy hat shading a charming smile as he towered over her five-foot-two-inch frame. As their gazes met, Alyssa was startled by the intensity of the man's blue eyes. "It's all right," she managed.

He released the grasp he had on her arm and held out his hand. "Nathan Cooper."

"Alyssa McCall," she said, smiling as she placed her much smaller hand into his. "You were in the restaurant."

He nodded. "It's one of my daughter's favorite places," he explained with a warm smile. "Best milk shakes around if you find you have a hankering for one."

She laughed softly. "I'll be sure to keep that in mind."

"Daddy, come on!" The excited cry was followed by the sound of bells tinkling as the store's door swung open.

Releasing her hand, his gaze shifted toward

the store. "I'd best get in there before my hyperactive little bull takes out the entire china shop."

"This is a china shop?" she replied in confusion.

"What?" he asked with a chuckle.

Alyssa's brow creased with worry. "I'm supposed to be at The Toy Box."

He studied her for a long moment before pointing to the sign that hung over the storefront. One that was little more than a blur to her. "You're in the right place. Largest mom and pop toy store in the county."

She let out a sigh of relief. "You had me worried for a minute." She reached for the handle of her suitcase, but he was faster.

"Allow me."

"There's no need—"

He held up his other hand, effectively cutting off her refusal of his help. "It's the least I can do after my daughter practically ran you over."

She relented, allowing him to carry her suitcase for her. And he didn't stop there. He opened the door and held it, motioning her inside.

"Thank you," she said as she moved past him into the store. If everyone in Braxton was as kind as Nathan Cooper, her stay would be far easier than she'd prayed it would be.

# Chapter Two

"You aren't by any chance a traveling Slinky sales rep, are you?" Nathan Cooper asked as he followed Alyssa inside.

"Excuse me?"

"The suitcase," he said, with a charming grin. "I'm guessing you're in toy sales of some sort."

She laughed softly at his teasing. "Not even close. I'm here to see Mr. Clark."

He nodded.

"Look, Daddy!" his daughter exclaimed as she pointed to the collection of animated figurines strategically placed in the storefront window. "It's Rudolph."

Alyssa stepped closer to watch the musical display. "You know, Rudolph's story was first told by Robert L. May in 1939 in a booklet he created for a department store called Montgomery Ward. That was over seventy years ago."

The little girl tipped her tiny face upward in wide-eyed amazement. "Rudolph's that old?"

"The story is that old," Alyssa explained with a smile. "But Rudolph is a very special reindeer," Alyssa said. "He doesn't get old. In fact, none of Santa's reindeer do."

"Because they're special, too!" Katie exclaimed.

Alyssa nodded. "That's right."

Nathan called out to his daughter. "We don't have much time, Cupcake. You'd best get started on that list."

His daughter, needing no more coaxing, scurried away to disappear between the aisles. Alyssa had spent enough time in physical therapy not to miss the slight limp to the little girl's gait. Probably nothing more than a bruised knee, but it brought Alyssa back to a time in her life she'd just as soon forget.

She turned to the girl's father. "I'm sorry. I didn't mean to distract her."

His gaze shifted in the direction his daughter had gone. "It's all right. Katie tends to get sidetracked easily and we don't have much time. I have to get back to work soon."

"Daddy, look at this!" His daughter hopped across the wood floor on a white stick pony.

Nathan Cooper smiled at her lovingly. "You're a regular cowgirl."

"Can I have it?"

"Not today, Cupcake, but we'll put it on the list."

"We can't put it on the list until you try it," she told him, worry creasing her tiny face.

"Me?" he replied, clearly confused by her request. "Why would I need to try it?"

"To know if it's a good horse or not."

"Honey…"

"Please, Daddy. You know everything about horses."

He glanced in Alyssa's direction. "I'm keeping you from your appointment."

"I'm a few minutes early, actually."

"You'll probably find Rusty in the back room, watching The Weather Channel."

Her smile faded. "Why? Are you expecting bad weather?" That would make getting around on foot so much harder.

He shook his head. "Nothing more than a light, though undoubtedly cold rain. And not until later this evening. Rusty just likes keeping up-to-date when it comes to the weather." That said, he reached for the toy pony his daughter was holding out to him.

Completely understandable, she thought, considering what the town had gone through. Reaching out, she retrieved the handle of her suitcase from his grasp. "Thank you so much for your help."

"My pleasure," he told her with a tip of his coal-black cowboy hat. One just as dark as the five-o'clock shadow on his firm jaw and midnight hair.

She parked her suitcase up against the wall next to the opening that led to the store's back room. A glance back over her shoulder found Nathan Cooper straddling the painted stick. His large frame making the toy appear even smaller.

He raised the horse's head with an impressively realistic whinny, eliciting laughter from his little girl and a smile from Alyssa. Turning away, she stepped into the smaller room in search of Mr. Clark.

Having seen the playful, loving interaction between Nathan Cooper and his young daughter, she now knew what a true knight on a white horse was. Even if this particular knight was dressed in blue jeans and a flannel shirt and the horse had mop strings for hair.

"Mr. Clark?"

The leather chair creaked in protest as it spun away from the paper-strewn desk. A compact television with The Weather Channel playing on it sat atop a smaller table next to the desk.

"Forgive me," the older man apologized as he pushed his portly form out of the chair. "I didn't hear the front bell ring. Then again my hearing hasn't been the same since the tornado."

"It's quite all right," Alyssa replied with an empathetic smile, speaking slightly louder than she had been. She stepped forward, extending her hand. "I'm Alyssa McCall. We spoke on the phone."

"Ah, yes," he replied with a nod as he shook her hand in greeting. "So glad to have you here."

"I'm thrilled to be a part of this." More than he could ever know.

He stepped past her to a small table by the window to pour himself some coffee. "Would you care for some?"

"No, thank you." It was too late in the day for caffeine. She'd be up all night. And after the keyed-up day she'd had so far, she was going to require a good night's sleep in order to give her all to the job the next morning.

"Your firm's offer to help out with the finishing touches on the recreation center was quite generous, Mrs. McCall. On behalf of the town council, we are truly grateful."

"It's Miss," she gently corrected. "And my company was more than glad to be of part of such a positive undertaking for your community."

"I have to admit," he began as he took a sip of the coffee he'd just poured himself, "that we never expected to have a professional interior designer join us on this project. I'm beyond thrilled."

She just hoped he wouldn't be disappointed. While she wanted to believe her skills were still sharp, not having as much opportunity to make use of those skills as she once had meant there was a possibility that her expertise might have diminished somewhat.

"Miss McCall?"

Alyssa snapped out of her thoughts with an apologetic smile. "Yes?"

"I was just saying that Myrna and Doris have a room for you over at The Cat's Cradle."

"The Cat's Cradle?"

"It's the boardinghouse they run at the far end of town. I'm sure you're aware the town agreed to take care of your accommodations during your stay here. The Wilson sisters have very generously offered to provide your lodgings at no cost to the town."

"That's so kind of them, but isn't renting rooms at the boardinghouse their livelihood? I'm more than willing to pay for my stay there."

"Nonsense." He waved the suggestion off. "In fact, the council already offered to pay them, but they refused to accept any money. This is their contribution to the rebuilding of our town. Besides, those two run the boardinghouse because they rarely venture away from The Cat's Cradle and welcome any and all company that comes their way. Neither one of them is in need of money. Trust me."

So far every person she had met or heard about in Braxton was unbelievably kind and giving. That eased her worries about being in a town where she knew no one. "I look forward to meeting them."

"I'm sure that goes both ways." The words had barely left his mouth when his smile faded, replaced by a worried frown. "You aren't allergic to cats are you?"

She shook her head. "Not that I know of. Why?"

"Because Doris has a real soft spot for felines." He started back to his desk. "I'll call and let them know you're on your way. You can stop by the rec center in the morning to see how things are coming along and decide on its finishing touches. Light fixtures, paint, trim and furniture of some sort."

"I'd like that. Is the boardinghouse within walking distance?"

"Maybe when the sun's shining. But there's the possibility of rain moving in. You'd be better off driving there."

"I'm afraid I don't own a car."

"Then how on earth did you get here?"

"A friend of mine drove me here," she explained. "She'll be back to pick me up once the job is finished."

"Which should be just in time for our annual Christmas Eve celebration. You and your friend are welcome to join us for it if you have the time. And while I'm at it, I would highly recommend seeing the reenactment of our Savior's birth the local church here puts on Christmas Eve afternoon. Brings tears to a grown man's eyes I tell you."

"It sounds wonderful. But Erica has family in San Antonio she'll be spending time with over the holidays. She's not scheduled to pick me up until the day after Christmas. But even if she can't make it for the church's program, I'll be certain not to miss it."

He sipped at the steaming coffee, studying her curiously. "No holiday plans for you?"

She lowered her gaze to the papers on his desk. "No."

"Well, we're glad to have you join us here in Braxton for the holidays."

"Thank you, Mr. Clark. I really appreciate that," she told him with a smile. "Now, can you tell me how to get to The Cat's Cradle?"

Rusty Clark's gaze shifted past her and a smile moved across his weathered face. "This here young man can take you there."

She turned to find Nathan Cooper's broad shoulders filling the open doorway.

"Take her where?" the cowboy replied, his gaze meeting hers.

"To The Cat's Cradle," the elderly store owner said. "Now that the sun's gone down, it's sure to be too cold for our town's guest to be walking that far."

Nathan nodded. "You'll get no argument from me there."

"I don't mind the cold," she insisted. "Besides, I'd rather not impose."

"It's no imposition" came his husky reply.

"*Miss* McCall," Rusty said, "I'd like you to meet Nathan Cooper."

"We've already met," she said, her gaze fixed on the man in the doorway. His face wasn't as clear as it had been when she'd looked up at him out on the sidewalk outside, but that didn't matter. She recalled every chiseled contour of his handsome face. The startling blue of his eyes. The slightly crooked hitch of his smile.

Rusty Clark clapped his hands together. "Wonderful. It saves me the time of making introductions. Something tells me the two of you are gonna work real good together."

"We'll what?" Both Nathan and Alyssa replied in unison.

"I assumed you already knew, seeing as how

the two of you are already acquainted. Nathan and his brother's company is in charge of construction for the rec center."

She looked his way. "I had no idea. I'm looking forward to seeing what you've done so far. I can't wait to start on the design plans for it."

Nathan Cooper held up a hand. "Hold up. Design plans?" He shot a questioning look in the older man's direction.

"Miss McCall's design firm has ever so generously offered to donate their services for the project and have sent us one of their top designers to do the job."

"I thought I was handling the project through to completion," he replied as he moved farther into the room to join them. "Does the council have some sort of problem with the work I've done so far?"

Mr. Clark shook his head. "Goodness, no. Your work, as usual, has been top-notch."

Alyssa bit at her bottom lip. She hadn't meant to step on anyone's toes when she'd accepted her firm's offer to send her to Braxton for this project. "If my helping out is gonna be a problem…"

"Nonsense," the councilman assured her. "Your assistance is more than welcome here. Nathan has already given this town so much of his time when it comes to the rebuilding efforts, accepting your offer was the least I could do for him."

"You might have let me know sooner," the glowering cowboy replied stiffly, his entire demeanor changing.

"Her firm only contacted me a few days ago with their very kind offer," Mr. Clark explained. "I had hoped to surprise you."

"Well, you succeeded." Some of the harshness in Nathan Cooper's expression faded as he looked her way. "Welcome to the team."

"Thank you."

"Now that we have that settled, what brings you here?" Mr. Clark inquired of Nathan. "Problem at the site?"

Nathan shook his head. "No. We're moving right along, all things considered. I just stopped by with Katie so she could add a few dozen more things to her Christmas list."

The older man chuckled. "Just like her moth…" His words trailed off.

A deafening silence fell in the room.

Alyssa looked between the two men, unsure of what had just happened. The tension in the air was palpable.

"I really should be getting back to work," Nathan said, breaking the uncomfortable silence. He turned to her. "Miss McCall?"

"Alyssa, please," she replied. "And I'm ready to leave whenever you are."

"We'll talk more tomorrow," Mr. Clark told her as he walked them out to the front of the store.

"I look forward to it." She reached for the handle of her suitcase only to find a much larger hand already wrapped around it—again. The warmth of his skin soothed her chilled fingers. Glancing up, she found Nathan Cooper staring down at her.

"Allow me."

"Thank you, but I think I'll walk to the boardinghouse after all. The crisp air will do me good."

He shrugged his broad shoulders, looking almost relieved. "Suit yourself."

Releasing his hold on her suitcase, Nathan tipped his hat, then turned toward the aisles of toys. "Let's go, Cupcake," he hollered. "Daddy's gotta get back to work."

A tiny whine floated through the air somewhere in the vicinity of the doll aisle. "But I'm not done yet," his daughter said as she stepped into view.

"We'll come back another time," he assured her. Right now he just had to get out of there. Away from the festive holiday music and mechanical Christmas characters. Away from the woman who was going to invade his life and stir up memories he'd just as soon forget.

He flexed his hand. The one she'd touched briefly. A light, gentle touch. Accidental. But it had been so long since he'd had any sort of physical contact with anyone other than his daughter it had taken him completely off guard.

"Daddy, what's this?" his daughter inquired as she skipped up to him.

He stared at the sprig of green tied with a red bow, which she held pinched between her fingers. "It's mistletoe."

"Whose toe?"

Alyssa McCall's soft laughter filled the room. "It's called mistletoe. Back in eighteenth-century England, if a young woman stood under some mistletoe, brightly trimmed with ribbons, she couldn't refuse to be kissed. In many cases, that special kiss under the mistletoe led to love and marriage."

Nathan stared at her in disbelief. Was the woman a walking encyclopedia on holiday traditions?

"It can make people fall in love?" Katie repeated in awe.

Miss McCall nodded. "So they say. Apparently, there's something very special and romantic about mistletoe."

"Can we buy some, Daddy?"

"Not today." *Or ever.* "Now go put that back where you found it and let's get going."

She scowled as she returned the sprig of mistletoe to its hook on the aisle's end cap display.

"I'd reconsider taking that ride with Nathan to the boardinghouse," Mr. Clark advised Alyssa as she neared the door, pulling her suitcase behind her. "It's gonna be a mighty cold walk to the other end of town."

"In the rain," Katie added as she bounced over to press her nose against the store's front window.

"It's raining?" the woman who had so unsettled Nathan gasped.

"Big fat drops!" his daughter exclaimed.

Alyssa looked his way.

Nathan shrugged. "Looks like they were wrong about the rain not moving in until later."

"Oh, no."

"My offer still stands."

"If you don't mind," she replied, looking less than thrilled.

"We don't mind a bit," Katie answered for him as she opened the door, letting a gust of wind-blown rain inside. "Daddy's got a real big truck with a real big seat."

Rusty's hearty chuckle followed them out the door.

Nathan swept Katie up in his arms, carrying her out to the truck. The last thing they needed was for her to slip on the wet sidewalk and re-injure her bad leg.

"How old are you?" his daughter asked Miss McCall as they settled into the truck's roomy cab.

"Katie," Nathan admonished. Was there ever a more inquisitive child?

"It's okay," Alyssa McCall replied with a smile. "I'm used to dealing with children's questions. I teach art at a recreational center back in San Antonio."

Her reply took him off guard. "I must have misunderstood. I thought Rusty said you were an interior designer."

"I am. I have my degree as well as plenty of work experience in the field. However, I'm only working part-time in interior design at the present." She glanced down at Katie. "And to answer your question, I'm twenty-seven."

"Are you married?"

"Katie Marie!" he gently reprimanded, staring down at his too-curious-for-her-own-good little girl who was seated on the bench seat between them.

The question didn't seem to daunt Miss McCall who answered with a simple, "No, Katie, I'm not."

"My daddy's—"

"Here we are," Nathan announced, effectively cutting off his daughter's reply. The large wooden sign welcoming guests to The Cat's Cradle swung in the cold, wet, winter wind. It was a welcome sight as he turned into the half-circle drive. A second later, he was pulling up in front of the old Victorian boardinghouse.

Katie squirmed in the seat. "It's the kitty house!"

"She has a thing for cats," he explained.

Miss McCall looked down at his daughter. "Me, too."

"Do you have a kitty of your own?" Katie asked, curiosity lighting her eyes.

"I'm afraid not. No pets are allowed in the town house I rent back in San Antonio."

"I don't have a pet either," his daughter said with a sigh. "Daddy's afraid—"

Nathan cleared his throat, cutting in. "I really do have to get back to work." He had to make certain the rec center was completed in time. Not so much for the Christmas Eve party that was to be held there, but for the dedication ceremony that would open the festivities, honoring those lost in the storm. He hadn't been there for Isabel that day, but he would be there to see the project through and his wife's memory honored.

"Of course," Miss McCall said apologetically. "I'm so sorry for throwing you off schedule."

"It's not a problem," he replied as he swung open the driver's side door. "Wait here, Cupcake. I'm gonna get Miss McCall's suitcase and then see her to the door."

"I wanna see the kitties."

"Another time, honey," he said, ruffling her hair. "Uncle Carter is waiting for Daddy to come help him with the rec center."

She let out an exaggerated sigh. "Okay."

"You don't have to see me to the door," Miss McCall told him. "I'll just grab my suitcase and you can go."

"Daddy doesn't mind helping you," his daughter cut in before he had a chance to reply. "He has really big muscles."

Miss McCall met his gaze, the corners of her mouth twitching as if trying very hard to suppress a grin. "Well, then, I guess I should let your daddy help me."

"Will I get to see you again?" his daughter asked, a little too eagerly for Nathan's comfort.

Alyssa offered her a warm smile. "You can pretty much count on it."

Not if he could help it. Not with Katie in mommy search mode. Nathan stepped out into the rain and rounded the truck. Opening the tailgate, he pulled her suitcase out from beneath the covered bed.

"Thank you for the ride," she said as she stepped up beside him, attempting to shield the both of them from the rain with the floral print umbrella she held clutched in her hand.

"Thank you for handling my daughter's meddling questions so well," he said as he walked her up the wet porch steps. Reaching out, he knocked on the door.

"Children are naturally curious. I didn't mind," she assured him as she lowered the umbrella to shake the excess rain from it. "You're blessed to have such an adorable little girl, curiosity and all."

"I tend to think so, but then my opinion might be a bit biased when it comes to my daughter."

She turned to look up at him. "About my helping out with the recreation center…"

A slight frown pulled at his mouth, try as he might to fight it. "Yes?"

"My intention in coming here was to do something to help your town," she said, closing the umbrella. "If that is gonna be a problem for you…"

"Don't trouble yourself any over that," he told her. "I'll deal with it."

# Chapter Three

*He'd deal with it.* Not a very promising start to their working relationship. The door swung open before Alyssa had a chance to reply and a tall, slender woman with a beehive of silver hair waved them inside.

"Come on in out of the weather, you two. I'll heat some water up for tea. Something to take the chill off."

"Appreciate the offer, Doris," Nathan Cooper replied with a smile, "but I can't stay. I'm just dropping Miss McCall here off."

The older woman looked to Alyssa. "Myrna and I have been expecting you. Rusty called to let us know you were on your way. Welcome to The Cat's Cradle."

"Thank you for having me," she said, propping her wet umbrella against the porch wall next to the door before stepping inside.

"It's our pleasure," Doris said, her gaze shifting to Nathan. "Are you sure you can't stay for tea?"

Nathan set her suitcase down in the front foyer. "Katie's waiting for me in the truck. I have to run her out to Mildred's place before I head back to work."

"Just be careful on those roads," Doris warned. "It's really coming down hard out there."

"You can count on it." His gaze shifted to Alyssa. "Guess I'll be seeing you tomorrow."

She nodded, then stood watching as the blurred outline of Nathan Cooper faded away behind a curtain of rain.

"A fine-looking young man, that one," Doris muttered behind her.

She turned from the window. "I was watching the rain."

"Of course you were, dear." She turned toward the winding oak staircase and cupped her hands to her mouth. "Myrna! Our guest is here."

Maybe she had been admiring the way Nathan Cooper carried himself, but that was it. She was there to do a job. Not to start something up with a man on the divorce rebound. Katie would just have to look elsewhere for someone for her daddy.

An elderly woman wearing a bright floral

housecoat and fuzzy pink slippers came scurrying down the stairs. "Miss McCall!"

"Call me Alyssa, please."

Myrna stood before Alyssa, a welcoming smile parting her wrinkled cheeks. Her blue-gray hair hung in a single braid over one shoulder. "We're so happy to have you staying here with us."

"Indeed," Doris agreed with a nod. "Braxton isn't exactly the tourist capital of Texas."

A fluffy white ball shot down the stairs and past their legs, disappearing into an adjoining room.

Myrna laughed. "That blur of white is the newest addition to our family, Bluebell."

"You like cats, don't you?" Doris asked.

Alyssa nodded. "Yes, I do." Although she'd never had one of her own.

"Good, because our dear little ones tend to crave affection."

She could relate to their need.

"You have the prettiest eyes," Doris observed, then leaned closer in her inspection of them.

*Too bad they didn't work.* That wasn't exactly true. Her eyes were perfect. The visual cortex part of her brain, which had been damaged in the accident, was the reason for her visual impairment.

Myrna leaned closer, as well, inspecting

Alyssa's eyes through her glasses. "She does. They're just like topaz under the sun."

"Goes well with her hair color."

Doris nodded. "I always thought green eyes complimented auburn hair the best, but I do believe I was wrong."

Alyssa blushed at their compliments and their close scrutiny. "You're both too sweet."

Just then two kittens with calico markings scampered into the entryway. Doris bent to pick them up. "This is Rhett and his favorite girl, Scarlett."

"Well, hello there," Alyssa said, scratching each of them behind their ears.

"Come on, dear," Doris said. "Let me give you a quick tour of the downstairs. Then I'll show you to your room."

"I'd like that."

"I'll go put some water on for tea," Myrna called out as Doris led her into the parlor.

The house was purely Victorian, from the striped damask curtains to the countless gilded picture frames that lined the walls. Taking a walk through the rooms helped Alyssa familiarize herself with the house's layout. Like Alyssa's town house, the women's home was filled with warm, white lights and holiday decor.

When the tour ended, Doris led her upstairs to the room she'd be staying in. Alyssa stepped inside and looked around, her gaze drawn to the off-white, antique cast-iron bed. She walked over to it, running her fingers over the faded beige ribbon-threaded quilt.

"Our mother made it," the older woman announced behind her.

"It's beautiful."

"She loved quilting. Unfortunately, neither Myrna nor I inherited our mother's sewing abilities," she said, a hint of sadness in her voice.

Alyssa turned to face her. "We all have our own special abilities. You and Myrna run a boardinghouse, and yet you still find time to take in strays and love them unconditionally. It's more than some children can say about their own parents." The second the words left her mouth, Alyssa wished she could take them back.

"Your parents didn't show you love?"

"I was simply making a reference," Alyssa replied with a nervous laugh.

"Of course you were," Doris said from the open doorway. "If you ever need to talk, dear, Myrna and I are very good listeners. Now you go get settled in and then come down to the kitchen and join us for a cup of tea."

"I'll do that. Thank you." Tears pricked at the backs of her eyes as the older woman stepped from the room, closing the door behind her. No, she would not think about her mother and the love she'd never been able to show Alyssa. That was something that would never change. Her mother was gone now, so there was no use wishing for what could never be.

Instead, she would strive to focus on only the good things God had blessed her with in Braxton. Like the kindhearted sisters who had so generously opened their home to her. Like the adorably inquisitive Katie Cooper and her stick-pony-riding father.

Nathan glanced toward his daughter, who appeared to be thoroughly captivated by the rain outside. As long as it wasn't storming with gusting winds, she was fine. Let the wind pick up and Katie became panicked. Understandable, all things considered.

He thought back to what she'd said earlier. Since losing her mother, Katie had never once voiced her discontent with the way things were. He'd assumed that Mildred's presence in her life, and then that of Audra's, satisfied any need his daughter might have for a mother figure. And maybe it had in the past, but something had changed. His little girl was looking for a mom.

That tugged at his heart. He would give his daughter the world if he could, but giving her another mother was asking for more than he was ready to do. And what if he did remarry again, for Katie's sake, and things didn't work out? Where would that leave his daughter? Motherless again. Heartbroken. Emotionally withdrawn. No, it wasn't worth the risk.

So how was he supposed to handle this situation? Ignore it? Tell Katie to stop wishing for what she could never have? It was moments like this that he missed Isabel the most. She always knew the right thing to say.

He pulled up to Mildred's place and shifted the truck into Park.

"Daddy, look how big the puddles are outside," Katie exclaimed, her lightly freckled nose pressed against the passenger window.

"It's coming down in bucketfuls," he acknowledged with a nod. Crazy weather patterns. High sixties and sunshine that afternoon. Cold rain that evening.

"I wanna jump in them."

At least his daughter's thoughts had moved on to something other than Alyssa McCall's marital status. He tossed his partially soaked cowboy hat onto the backseat to dry, then stepped out into the rain. As he rounded the back of the truck, he shrugged out of his coat. Then, opening the passenger door, he gathered his daughter up in his arms, wrapping her up in his coat to shield her from the rain's onslaught. "The winds are picking up. We don't want you blowing away."

Katie stiffened in his arms with a muffled gasp. "I don't wanna be blown away," she cried out, her arms clutching his neck.

He mentally chastised himself for his careless choice of words. He tightened his hold on her with a sigh. "Don't you worry, honey, Daddy would never let that happen to you."

"But it happened to Mommy."

And there wasn't a day that went by that he didn't blame himself for Isabel's death. He'd been off with his brothers working on a job site. He hadn't been there when his family had needed him the most.

Before he had a chance to reply, the front door swung open and Mildred walked out. "There you two are. I was beginning to worry."

He set Katie on her feet. "We had to swing by The Cat's Cradle first."

"Yeah," Katie joined in, her mood shifting back to its normal carefree state. "We had to give Alyssa a ride there."

"*Miss* McCall," Nathan corrected as he shoved a hand back through his wet hair.

"Miss McCall?"

He nodded. "Apparently, she's gonna be helping out with the decorative touches to the rec center."

"She's real pretty," his daughter added with a glance in his direction.

The older woman smiled, her gaze shifting to Nathan, as well. "Oh, is she now?"

He shrugged. "I didn't pay that much attention." But he had. Enough to know that Alyssa's hair was an unusual shade of red-gold that seemed to come to life under the light. Enough to know that her thick lashes framed eyes the color of warm honey.

"I see," the older woman said, but her expression said that she didn't quite believe him. "Come on in out of that rain and you can tell me all about this Miss McCall."

"I'm soaked clean through," he said, nudging his daughter into the warmth of Mildred's house. "I need to swing by the house and pick up some dry clothes before I head back to work." What he failed to add was that Miss McCall was the last person he wanted to talk about. She was invading his thoughts with those honey-colored eyes and disarming smile, and was taking over part of the job he should have been overseeing and making his daughter want things, like a new mother, even more, which she couldn't have. Reaching out, he ruffled his daughter's hair. "I should be back to pick Katie up around nine thirty."

"Why don't you just leave Katie here for the night? No sense traveling on these roads any more than you have to on an evening like this."

Katie clapped her hands together. "Can I stay, Daddy? Please! Please!"

Mildred was right. The rain coming down as hard and fast as it was could make for unexpected flash floods. Better safe than sorry. "All right, Cupcake. I'll swing by at lunch tomorrow to check on you."

"Yippee!"

He bent to kiss the top of her baby-fine hair and then straightened, turning to Mildred. "Call my cell if you need me."

"We'll be fine. You just concentrate on getting the rec center done. The town is counting on you."

He nodded. "I'm doing my best."

He was the kind of man who put his heart into every job, but this time was different. Every minute, no every second he spent working toward finishing the rec center in time for the town's Christmas Eve party was a painful reminder of what he and Katie had lost. Of the Christmases they would no longer share as a complete and happy family.

Despite the turmoil that filled him, he had committed himself to seeing the job through. At least, as far as the building's structure was concerned. Rusty had procured help putting up the holiday trimmings from the church's Bible group as well as the local ladies' bingo club. Katie would go to the party with Nathan's brother Carter and Audra and their kids, allowing him to avoid all that holiday cheer. Then afterward, they'd drop Katie off at home and the two of them would have a quiet Christmas Eve at home, just the two of them.

Pushing all thoughts of Christmas aside, Nathan turned his focus back to the road ahead. Water covering the pavement made hydroplaning a possibility. He eased up on the gas as he drove down the wet road. Leaving Katie at Mildred's for the night had definitely been a wise decision.

As soon as he arrived at his place, Nathan called Carter, leaving a message on his brother's cell phone that he was on his way. Then he hurried upstairs to his room to change out of his wet clothes.

When he finally arrived at the rec center, nearly half an hour later, Nathan slid out of the warmth of his truck and back into the cold, wet rain. Raising the collar of the dry coat he'd switched over to, he hurried across the rain-soaked parking area to the newly erected building. One that housed an indoor swimming pool, a TV and game room, an arts and craft room as well as several other recreation-devoted rooms. In the spring, once the weather cleared, an outdoor basketball court, a couple of shuffleboard courts and several picnic tables would be added.

He swung open the front door of the newly constructed building and stepped inside. Removing his jacket, he hung it over a nearby sawhorse, set his still-damp cowboy hat atop it and then moved farther into the room, spotting his brother atop a ladder. "Sorry I'm late."

"Don't apologize," Carter called down from his perch where he stood working on the wiring for one of the overhead lights. "You've been working day and night to get this job done. Katie needs you, too."

*No, what Katie needs is a mommy*, Nathan thought, his daughter's words having burrowed themselves under his skin like a thorn.

"How is my little Katydid?" his brother asked as he moved down the ladder.

"Lively as usual," he muttered, looking around. "Where's the crew?"

"In the arts and crafts room, finishing the trim on the windows."

Nathan nodded distractedly.

"Something troubling you?" Carter asked as he walked over to join him. Just a year younger than Nathan, Carter had always been able to read his moods. Their momma used to tell them they were meant to be twins, only Carter decided to hold out a year longer before making his own grand entrance into the world.

"No," he muttered. "Why?"

His brother snorted. "You always were a poor liar. What's going on?"

Nathan stepped past him to collect his tool belt from the eight-foot folding table that held an array of power tools along with several boxes of nails and drywall screws. "Katie wants a new mother," he said with a sigh as he slung the leather belt around his waist and buckled it.

"What?" his brother choked, sounding every bit as surprised as he'd been.

He turned with a frown. "That's what my daughter wants for Christmas. A mother. She even went so far as to give her own little 'mommy interview' to this woman who just arrived in town."

His brother shook his head with a sigh. "Tough one. Not that I don't understand Katie's wanting a mother in her life. I reckon a girl needs that."

"She has Mildred and Audra. That's as close as she's gonna get to having a mother figure in her life. Speaking of which, how is Audra doing?"

His brother's face beamed at the question. "She's holding up. The morning sickness tends to get the better of her, but knowing the wondrous gift we're gonna have soon helps get her through the day. The doctor says the nausea should only last another month or so."

"Glad to hear it. You couldn't have chosen a better mother for your child." Audra had given up everything she'd known to move to Braxton with her children after her husband divorced her, abandoning his children in the process. She was determined to give them a better life. Then she met his brother and they fell in love, giving her children the true family they had always wanted.

"Agreed," Carter said, a hint of heartfelt emotion pulling at his voice. "Getting back to Katie's request for a momma. She's too young to understand what you went through when you lost Isabel. But I do. I remember praying for you every day. Wishing I could do something to bring back the brother I knew. One who used to live life to its fullest. Who smiled often. And loved completely."

"Carter—"

His brother held up a hand, cutting him off. "I don't blame you for being afraid of letting someone else into your heart." Reaching out, he clasped a hand atop his brother's shoulder. "I saw what losing Isabel did to you. I had no intention of ever putting myself in that position. But then the Lord brought Audra into my life and I couldn't keep myself from loving her. Our daddy was right. We have to have faith. In ourselves. In our love. And, more importantly, in the Lord's plan for us."

Their father had told them from his deathbed in the hospital, *Have faith. There is always hope beyond the storm.* Despite those weakly uttered last words, all three of Caldwell Cooper's sons had decided that day that faith wasn't enough. If it had been, their loved ones would still be there. They'd made a pact that none of them would ever take the risk of loving and losing again. Katie was the only exception to their rule. She was already a part of their lives and needed all the love they could give her. Then Carter had to go and let his heart get in the way of common sense. But Nathan understood. Audra was a woman worth loving and she had given her heart completely to his brother.

"So tell me about this woman our little Katie interrogated," his brother said, lifting an arm to wipe the sweat from his brow with the sleeve of his flannel shirt.

"She's from San Antonio," Nathan told him. "Apparently, she's an interior designer. Her company offered to send her here pro bono to help with the finishing touches to the rec center."

His brother arched a questioning brow. "Rusty accepted that without consulting us?"

He nodded.

"I thought we were supposed to be handling the entire project," Carter muttered, clearly ruffled by Rusty's lack of communication with them on the matter.

"So did I."

His brother shrugged. "Reckon we can use all the help we can get if we wanna get the rec center completely finished in time. I just wish Rusty had given us some notice."

"From what I understand, this was a last-minute offer." His frown deepened. "Apparently Alyssa has a degree and several years experience, and the board jumped at the chance to have her join in on the project—"

"Alyssa?" his brother cut in, his dark brow arching even further.

"Alyssa McCall. That's her name," Nathan stated matter-of-factly. "As I was saying, she has expertise in interior design and Rusty jumped at the opportunity to have her handle that part of the project."

His brother stroked his whisker-stubbled chin in thought, then let his hand fall away with a casual shrug. "I suppose it's all for the same cause and she does have a degree..."

"We don't need her help," Nathan muttered in irritation. Making decisions on the final touches for a lot of their jobs had once been Isabel's responsibility. She hadn't needed some fancy degree to make everything come together. She was a natural. Now he and Carter, along with whoever was contracting their construction services, made those decisions.

"Look at it this way," his brother said, understanding in his eyes. "It'll free up a little more time for you to spend with Katie instead of spending it all here."

Nathan scoffed. "You're beginning to sound like Mildred."

"She must be rubbing off on me," his brother said with a grin. "So, is she pretty?"

"Mildred?"

Carter rolled his eyes. "I already know what a pretty gal Millie is. I was referring to Miss McCall. More important, is she single?"

Nathan groaned. "I've just figured out where Katie gets her nosy nature from."

"I wasn't asking for you. I was asking for Logan."

"Our brother happens to be a confirmed bachelor," he replied with a frown.

His brother eyed him curiously.

"What?" Nathan demanded.

"The little lady caught your eye," Carter accused, his grin widening. "That's why you're so bristly about her being here. She must be a pretty one."

Nathan's patience with the conversation ended. "I don't care how pretty she is. The only woman I ever loved is gone. I'm not looking to replace her. So stop—" his words were cut off by the ringing of his cell phone.

Pulling it from his jeans pocket, he glanced down at the caller ID and then back at his brother. "It's Millie," he said.

His brother nodded, stepping away while he took the call.

"Hello?"

"Nathan," Mildred said, her voice quivering. "I'm sorry to bother you at work."

The tremor in her voice had his heart dropping like a lead weight. "What's wrong?"

"I'm afraid there's been an emergency," she told him.

Despite their strength, his muscular legs threatened to give way beneath him. He struggled to take a breath. *Please, God, not again.*

Carter was beside him in an instant. "What is it, Nathan?"

He waved his brother off and forced the dreaded question from his suddenly bone-dry mouth. "Is it Katie?"

"Oh, goodness, no. She's right as rain," Millie assured him. "It's my sister."

Relief swept through him with gale force. "Your sister," he repeated as he dragged a hand back through his hair. Then his thoughts shifted to concern for Millie, who had been through enough after losing her husband. "Is she all right?"

"From what I understand, Eleanor lost her balance coming down the stairs this evening and broke her ankle. It's bad enough to require immediate surgery, which they've scheduled for tomorrow."

"Ah, Millie," he said, shaking his head, "I hate to hear that. Is there anything I can do?"

"That's why I'm calling. Eleanor's all by herself. I really need to be there with her."

"Of course, you do," he said without even a moment's hesitation. "I'll come get Katie."

"No need to pick her up right now," Millie assured him. "She can sleep here tonight like we planned and you can pick her up in the morning. I'm not about to drive up to Laredo tonight. Not with the weather being what it is."

"I can drive you there," he offered. How could he not? Millie had done so much for him the past two years.

"I appreciate the offer," she said, "but Eleanor really needs to get some rest before her surgery tomorrow."

"Are you sure?"

"I'm sure. You just keep on working to get that rec center done in time for the party. I'll make a few calls and see if I can round up some-one to watch Katie until I get back. I'm not sure how long I'll be needed in Laredo."

"Don't trouble yourself any," he told her. "I'll just bring Katie into work with me tomorrow. There's no school. Some sort of teacher in-ser-vice day, which will be followed right after by Christmas break. I'm sure Audra would be will-ing to help out if I need her while you're away."

"Of course," she said. "Thank you for being so understanding about my leaving."

"Eleanor's your sister," he told her. "You need to be there for her. Now you be sure to get some rest yourself. I'll be by first thing tomorrow morning to pick Katie up."

"I'll have her ready."

"And, Millie…"

"Yes?"

"Give Katie a kiss good-night for me."

"I'll do that."

He turned the phone off and found Carter standing there staring at him.

"What happened?" his brother asked, his brows furrowed in concern.

"Millie's sister in Laredo busted her ankle pretty bad. She's having surgery tomorrow and Millie's gonna head on up there to be with her. Sounds like she'll be staying with her sister for a while afterward to help out."

"I have to admit, when you first answered her call and I saw the color drain from your face, I thought something had happened to Katie."

"You and me both," Nathan admitted. His baby girl was his world. If anything ever happened to her...

He forced the thought from his mind and pulled the hammer from its loop on his tool belt. "What are we standing around for? We've got us a rec center to finish."

# Chapter Four

The morning sun shone brightly through the multipaned windows of the dining room as Alyssa hurried downstairs, eager to start her day's work at the rec center.

"Good morning, dear," Doris greeted from the dining room, giving Alyssa a start.

"You're up early," she said. "I hope I didn't wake you."

"Not at all. I rise with the sun."

Just then, Myrna entered through a door on the far side of the room, a warm smile moving across her face. "Perfect timing," she said as she moved toward the antique pedestal table in the center of the room. In one hand, she held a bowl filled with what Alyssa guessed to be scrambled eggs. In the other, a plate of crispy bacon, which had Alyssa's mouth watering. "Come on in and have a seat, dear. We'll see to it you're fed before you start your busy workday."

Alyssa stepped into the room and settled into one of the balloon-backed Victorian chairs. "You didn't have to make me breakfast. I could have grabbed something on my way through town."

"Honey, this is a bed-and-breakfast," Doris reminded her as she and Myrna took their places at the table. "You can't have one without the other."

Myrna set the filled dishes in the center of the table and then reached for the vintage rose-print teapot. "Tea?"

Alyssa nodded. "Yes, please."

Lifting the delicate old teapot gingerly, she filled Alyssa's teacup with steaming water and then pushed a doily-lined wicker basket filled with assorted teas across the table to her.

"You were so tired last night," Myrna said as she dipped her tea bag up in down in her tea water, "that we decided not to bombard you with questions about yourself."

"There's not much to tell," Alyssa said as she perused her choices, selecting an apple-cinnamon tea. "I was born and raised by a single mother in Waco. No brothers or sisters. I never knew my father."

"I'm so sorry to hear that," Doris said with an empathetic frown.

Alyssa forced a smile. "Can't miss what you never had," she said. "After graduating from Baylor, I was offered a job with a large interior design firm down in San Antonio. So I packed up and moved south to begin my new life."

"Have you ever been on TV?" Doris asked as she spooned two heaping teaspoons of sugar into her cup.

Alyssa was thrown by the unexpected question. "TV?"

"You know," Myrna joined in. "On one of those home makeover shows you see all over television these days. You're sure pretty enough to be a TV star. Isn't she, Doris?"

Her sister nodded, the beehive of hair piled atop her head shifting to and fro. "I could see her starring in one of those cooking shows, looking all pretty in her ruffled apron."

Alyssa laughed softly. These two women were so endearing. "I'm afraid cooking is not my forte."

"All you really need to know how to make is sweets," Doris noted as she sipped at her tea. "My beloved Henry, God rest his soul, was especially fond of my sister's county-fair-winning apple-pecan cobbler." Her gaze drifted off and a soft smile lit her face. "That man had quite the sweet tooth."

"Most men do," Myrna said. "Nathan Cooper included. Just ask Millie."

"She's a close family friend," Myrna explained. "Always baking up sweets for those Cooper boys."

"Nathan...I mean Mr. Cooper," Alyssa quickly corrected, "has sons, too?"

"No, only Katie," Myrna clarified. "My sister was referring to Nathan and his two younger brothers, Carter and Logan. Big and strong, those boys. Some of the heartiest stock Texas produces."

"Like three peas in a pod," Myrna told her. "All with that same dark, wavy hair and bright blue eyes. Just like their daddy had. Real lookers, those Cooper boys."

If his brothers had even a smidgen of Nathan Cooper's good looks and charm, she could understand why even women old enough to be the men's grandmothers were smitten with them.

Huddled beneath the hood of her jacket, Alyssa quickened her step. The previous night's rain had left the earth damp and the air chilled. She should have thought to bring gloves with her when she packed for the trip. It would have made the long walk from the boardinghouse to the opposite end of town far more tolerable.

The moment she saw the large Cooper Construction sign flanking the front sidewalk of what had to be the town's new rec center, relief swept through her.

Picking up her step, she hurried toward the entrance. The warmth that greeted her when she stepped inside was a welcome respite from the chill outside. Pulling the door closed behind her, she brought her hands to her mouth, breathing warmth onto her very cold, very stiff fingers.

"You walked here?" a deep, familiar voice demanded behind her.

Startled, she turned to find Nathan Cooper watching her from a nearby doorway. Frown still intact. "How else was I supposed to get here?" she asked in her own defense. "Taxis don't exactly line the streets of Braxton."

"I could have given you a ride."

"The walk wasn't that bad."

"I suppose the tinge of blue in your lips is some sort of newfangled lipstick color?"

"They're blue?" she gasped, her chilled fingers flying to her lips.

"Close enough," he said as he joined her in what would, once finished, be the lobby area. His narrowed gaze traveled over her, then with a shake of his head he said, "Come on," motioning for her to follow him down a long hallway.

"Where are we going?" she asked as she unzipped her jacket.

"There's a space heater in the next room. You can warm up some before you get started doing whatever it is you do."

"That would be nice," she said, following him. It was all she could do to keep up with his long strides.

He pointed to an open doorway. "You can warm up in there." That said, he disappeared into another of the rooms that lined the hallway.

"Thank you," she called out after him. Then she stepped into the room he'd directed her to where several men were busily at work. One by one the sounds of hammers and drills stopped and she felt more than saw their gazes shift her way. Lifting her hand, she offered a nervous smile, hoping their dispositions would be a tad more welcoming than Nathan Cooper's had been. "Hello."

A man who had been running a nearby table saw walked over to where she stood by the door. He was wearing safety goggles, his dark, wavy hair brushing over the top of them. His height caused her to crane her neck as he stopped in front of her.

"Can I help you?"

"I'm Alyssa McCall."

Shoving the safety goggles off his face and onto his head, he studied her with a widening grin. "The interior designer?"

"That's what I have my degree in, but I also teach art classes to children at a recreation center in San Antonio, which is where I'm from. It's a job I enjoy immensely."

His gaze moved over her in an assessing manner. "When my brother told me you'd be joining us sometime this morning, he conveniently left off the part about your being…"

"My being what?"

He glanced toward the other workers before saying, his voice low, "Not old."

She stiffened at his response. "I can assure you I have plenty of design experience."

"I'm not doubting your skill," he said apologetically. "Let's try this again." Pulling off his leather work gloves, he extended a hand. "Carter Cooper. Co-owner of Cooper Construction. Welcome to the crew."

She took the offered hand. "Thank you."

His dark brow lifted. "Your hand's as cold as ice."

"I know. The walk here was a little chillier than I expected," she admitted.

"You walked here from the boardinghouse? It's clear on the other side of town."

She resisted the urge to roll her eyes at his stunned reaction. The walk hadn't been all that far. Not for someone who was used to walking nearly everywhere she went. The problem was having been underdressed for the inclement weather.

"I did," she replied. "Your brother sent me in here to warm up by the space heater."

"And here I am talking your ear off," he muttered with a frown. "Back to work," he hollered to the other workers. "Come on," he told her. "The space heater's over here."

She trailed after him, grateful when she felt the warmth from the portable heater start to curl around her. "So what exactly did your brother tell you about my being here?" she asked as she leaned in, shoving her hands closer to the heat.

He smiled. "He mentioned you'd be stopping by today."

"Much to his dismay, I'm sure," she murmured as the chill began to ease from her shivering limbs.

His husky chuckle filled the air. "Try not to take it personally, Miss McCall."

"It's a little hard not to," she said. "Your brother was all smiles and politeness when we first met, but the second he found out I was gonna be helping with the interior design portion of the recreation center, his demeanor toward me did a complete one-eighty."

"I'll talk to him," he assured her with a kind smile.

"I'd appreciate it. I truly do want the same thing you all do," Alyssa said. "To help give this town back some of what it lost in that storm."

"Miss McCall!" The high-pitched shriek echoed off the unpainted walls.

Alyssa glanced back over her shoulder to see Katie Cooper hurrying in her direction, the little girl's limp slightly more pronounced than it had been the evening before. "Katie," she said with a smile. "What a surprise finding you here this morning."

"Daddy just told me you were here. He had to bring me to work with him today."

"He did?" she said in surprise. "Is your mommy sick?"

"No," she replied, her beautiful smile sagging. "She went to Heaven with Grammy and Pappy."

Alyssa's heart wrenched. She'd assumed the day before that her father was divorced. Not for a second had she ever considered the possibility that he was widowed. Not at his age. She couldn't manage any kind of response. How could she when she had no idea what to say? Instead, she offered up a silent prayer for the Lord to watch over this dear, sweet, motherless child. And her father, as well.

"Hey, Katydid," Carter said from behind Alyssa, breaking the uncomfortable silence. "How would you like to give Miss McCall here a tour around the rec center?"

The little girl's face lit up once again. "Sure!"

Alyssa flashed him a grateful smile for saving the moment. Her heart ached for Katie. So very young to have lost her mother.

"You can hang your coat over there," Katie said. Her earlier bright smile back in place.

Pulled from her sympathetic musings, she looked to where Katie was pointing, but she could only make out shadowy outlines on the far side of the room.

"I think Miss McCall might wanna keep her coat on," the little girl's uncle cut in. "She's a little cold from outside."

"Actually, I'm feeling warmer already." Removing her coat, Alyssa crossed the room, stepping cautiously around worktables and over electrical cords. She scanned the area, relieved to spot several empty coat hooks on the wall by the door. She was still slightly chilled, but the building was decently heated.

"Come on," Katie said excitedly, holding out her hand.

Clasping her hand around Katie's, she smiled

down at her. "Lead the way, my little tour guide." She couldn't get Katie's sorrowful admission out of her mind. How unbearably tragic to think she'd had a mother who would have given the world to be there to guide her child. To raise her. To love her. Unlike Alyssa's own mother who'd thrown away that same chance.

"This is the ball room," Katie announced at their first stop.

Alyssa looked around as she withdrew her notepad from her purse. "You could fit a lot of dancers in here."

Katie giggled. "You're not supposed to be dancing while you're playing ball."

It took a moment for Katie's words to sink in. What had she been thinking? This was a rec center. A ball room in a recreation center would not be a ballroom. She needed to get her mind on her work instead of on things she couldn't change. But it wouldn't be easy. This little girl touched something deep inside her.

"There's gonna be basketball and volleyball and maybe even kickball in here," Katie continued on excitedly.

"Sounds like you're gonna have so much fun."

Her little smile sagged ever so slightly. "Not me."

"Why not?"

"'Cause I can't play ball," she answered with a frown.

"I'm sure your daddy could teach you."

She shook her head, her dark brown ponytails bouncing atop her slender shoulders. "He won't 'cause of my leg."

Alyssa didn't want to pry, but it seemed like Katie wanted to talk about it. "I noticed you were limping a little bit. Did you hurt your leg?"

"It got broken real bad."

That explained the slightly awkward gait. "Maybe when it's all better you can play kickball?"

"It is all better. As better as it's gonna be," she said. "I have a special piece in my leg. I have to be careful."

Katie must have had either had a rod or plate of some kind put in her leg. She recalled Nathan carrying Katie out of the store to the truck the night before. No doubt making sure she didn't slip and fall and possibly reinjure her leg. No wonder she felt a connection to this sweet, little girl.

"I have a special piece, too," she told her.

Katie's dark eyes widened. "You do?"

Alyssa nodded with a smile. "I sure do."

"In your leg?"

"No," she said. "Mine's in my head."

"Do people make fun of you for it?" the little girl asked timidly.

"Not many people know about it. Has someone said something to you about your leg that hurt your feelings?"

She hesitated, looking down at the floor. "Sometimes other kids say things…"

Alyssa knelt in front of her. "You know, Katie, sometimes people are scared of things they don't understand. They don't have special pieces inside them like we do, so they aren't sure how to react. Unfortunately, there are times when their reactions hurt our feelings."

"I suppose so," she mumbled.

Alyssa offered a comforting smile. "You know, sweetie, it's up to us to be strong when others get scared of our being special. We have to find ways to make them understand. To feel comfortable about our differences."

"I don't wanna be different," Katie whined, her mouth forming a tiny pout.

"You aren't different," Alyssa assured her. "You are wonderfully special."

"I am?"

She nodded emphatically. "Absolutely. Tell you what, how about you and I be strong together?"

"Forever?" she asked. The dark eyes looking up at Alyssa hopeful.

A part of her wanted to say yes, but she wouldn't be there forever. Only a few weeks. Less than that, if Nathan Cooper had his way. "I have to go home to San Antonio once I'm done helping your daddy with the rec center. But if you're ever having one of those days when you're sad because someone hurt your feelings, don't be afraid to talk to your daddy about it."

"But he might not understand 'cause he doesn't have any special parts."

"He'll understand. I promise," she said without hesitation. Having seen Nathan Cooper with his daughter, she had no doubt he would be able to give Katie the emotional support she needed. "Besides, I believe it was you who pointed out just how strong your daddy is. Isn't that right?"

Katie nodded.

"Then who better to help you to be strong than your daddy? Someone who loves you with all his heart." Unlike her own father, who'd chosen to go on with his own life without Alyssa ever being allowed in it.

Nathan stood in the doorway, taking in the scene before him. Katie and Alyssa's conversation had drifted out into the hall along with the sounds of construction being done in the room next to this one. It wasn't surprising that sound traveled so easily inside the newly erected building. Not with the flooring having yet to be laid, walls to be painted and doors to be hung.

His first instinct had been to go to his daughter and soothe her emotional hurts, but Alyssa McCall had done that for him. Surprisingly well, he had to admit. If what she'd told Katie about having her own special piece were true, then she truly understood what his daughter was going through.

He studied the woman comforting his daughter. She wasn't as tall as Isabel had been. And her hair was red. Not a bright red like the town's new fire truck. But a deeper, warmer red with hints of gold in it. He preferred dark hair like his wife's had been. But he had to admit the color seemed to suit Miss McCall. Warm. Soothing. Just as her words had been to his daughter.

"Thatta girl," Miss McCall said, giving his daughter's ponytail a playful tug. He watched as she rose up from the crouch she'd been in to smile down at Katie. "I can't wait to see everything your daddy's done so far. I understand he's been working very hard on the rec center."

"Granny Timmons says he's gonna work himself to the bone. I don't want my daddy to be a skeleton. They're scary."

Alyssa laughed softly. "I don't think that's what your granny meant by that. When people say someone is working themselves to the bone, what they're really trying to say is that the person is giving everything they have in them to do the best job they can. Your daddy is giving his all to have this place finished in time for the Christmas Eve festivities."

A smile pulled at his lips. He didn't want to be drawn to the woman who had been thrown into his life, into his neatly laid-out plans for the rec center, but watching her with his little girl, hearing her kind, reassuring words, did just that. Alyssa McCall affected him in a way no other woman had since Isabel.

"I wish Daddy didn't work so much," his daughter admitted with a sigh. "I miss him sometimes."

His daughter's words tugged at his heart. His attempt to bury himself in his work to forget the past had clearly left Katie feeling neglected. He'd never meant for that to happen.

"I'm sure he misses you, too," Miss McCall said, drawing him from his troubled thoughts. She still hadn't noticed him standing there. Probably a good thing, seeing as how he needed a moment to collect himself before making his presence known. She reached out, gently ruffling Katie's ever-wild mane of curls. "Just think of how happy your daddy's gonna make the people in town when they finally have their recreation center back. Now how about giving me a few minutes to take a peek around the room and then we can continue on with our tour?"

"Okay," Katie chirped. Leaving Alyssa to her work, his daughter set off across the expansive gymnasium floor, arms out wide, giggling as she twirled about in slow circles.

Alyssa McCall was something else. Despite his initial reservations, he felt himself softening toward her. That thought lasted all of about ten seconds as Miss McCall began her peek around the room, which appeared to be more of a thorough scrutiny of his work. Bristling, he watched as she moved about the room, running her fingertips over the recently sanded drywall sheets, pausing to examine each and every one of the multipaned windows and unstained door frames that lined the unfinished walls. Isabel had never questioned his ability.

"You can leave the drywall inspection to me," he said as he stepped up behind her.

Startled, she swung around to face him. "Mr. Cooper. I didn't see you come in."

"I'm not surprised," he grumbled. His gaze shifted to his daughter, who was at the far side of the unfinished gymnasium, and then back to Miss McCall. "Let's get one thing straight," he said, keeping his voice low. "Your job is to pick out paint colors and fixtures. Not to inspect my work."

"Inspect your work?" she replied, her expression one of confusion. Then her gaze fell to the drywall dust coating the tips of her fingers. "I…" She lifted her gaze to his.

"I'll do my job," he said brusquely. "You do yours."

"For your information," she began in a tone of forced patience, "I wasn't *inspecting* anything. I happen to be a very tactile person when I work. At least, I have been since—"

"Hi, Daddy!" Katie called out as she skipped over to join them.

His attention shifted to his daughter. "Hey, Cupcake."

"I got a job."

He arched a dark brow. "You do?"

"Uncle Carter asked me to give Miss McCall a tour," she said with a bright smile. "We're gonna go see the cafeteria next. Wanna come with us?"

Alyssa didn't give him a chance to reply. "I'm sure your daddy is far too busy to tag along."

He met her gaze, seeing a hint of hurt in her eyes. Why did the thought of that bother him? Maybe because he had been less than the gentleman his momma had raised him to be when setting her straight moments before. It wasn't her fault the firm she worked for had sent her there to do the job. The same job Isabel would have been handling if she were still alive.

"Daddy?"

Feeling as if the walls were closing in on him, he forced his attention back to his daughter. "Honey, I'd like to, but right now I have to—"

"*Please*, Daddy." Katie looked up at him with pleading brown eyes.

*Get it together, Cooper. Your daughter needs you.* And according to the conversation he'd overheard a few minutes ago, he hadn't been there enough for Katie during the past few months. "I suppose I could spare a few extra minutes for my favorite girl," he said, bringing a delighted smile to his daughter's face.

"Yay!" she exclaimed, and then she turned to Miss McCall. "Follow me! It's right next door."

"Careful!" he called after her with a worried frown. "I don't want you tripping on any power cords!"

"I won't!" she called back before disappearing through the open doorway.

"I wish I had half her energy," Miss McCall said as they started after her.

*Do the right thing*, his conscience told him. "Miss McCall," he said, stopping her just before they reached the framed-in doorway.

She turned to look up at him. "Look, I'm not here to step on your toes. Really I'm not. I can do most of my work from the boardinghouse on my computer if you'll email me a copy of the rec center's layout and measurements. Then you won't need to worry about having to cross paths w—"

He reached out to touch her arm, needing to explain that the problem wasn't her. It was him. "I'm sorry for making you feel like you aren't welcome here. It's just that I haven't worked with another woman since…" His words trailed off.

She reached up to curl her fingers around his hand, easing it away from her arm. "Since your wife passed away?" she asked softly.

His surprise must have shown on his face, because she added, "Katie told me."

"My daughter's a regular little chatterbox," he said, his voice tight with the emotion he fought to keep inside.

"I'm sorry for your loss."

He nodded, closing his eyes for a long moment before opening them to meet her softened gaze. "Isabel was in charge of the interior design portion of my company. She didn't have a fancy degree, but she knew how to make things work."

She didn't release his hand. Instead, she gave it a comforting squeeze. Eyes the color of amber searched his own. "I promise I'm not trying to replace her. I'm just here to do my job. But if my doing so is gonna be this hard on you, I'll pull out. The firm I work for can send a replacement. They have two men on their interior design staff. If one of them is free over the holidays…"

"No," he said, the words thick with emotion. "You need to stay."

She released his hand with a warm smile. "Okay."

Nathan cleared his throat, glancing around uneasily. Other than the overwhelming love he had for his daughter, this was the first time he'd really felt anything in the way of true emotion in two years.

"We should go," she said. "Katie will be wondering what happened to us."

"Before we go…" he said as he collected himself. "I wanna thank you."

"For what?"

"For being so kind to my daughter. I overheard the two of you discussing her leg."

"Mr. Cooper—" she began.

"Nathan," he cut in. "We're gonna be working together. No need for formalities between us."

She nodded. Her beautiful smile widening. "Agreed. Call me Alyssa, please. And you don't have to thank me for being kind to Katie. She's precious and endearing. And I understand what she's going through more than most people."

"Because of the plate you have in your head?" he said, wanting her to know that he'd been listening to their conversation longer than he should have before making his presence known. Another thing his momma would have taken him to task for.

"That's part of it," she said, biting at her bottom lip as if wanting to say more.

What more could there be? And then it occurred to him. "You lost your mother at a young age, as well?"

"Although my mother has been lost to me for most of my life, she only recently passed away," she explained. "She was an alcoholic."

"I'm sorry."

"Don't be. God has a plan for my life," she explained with a conviction he found himself wishing he still had when it came to the Lord. "In fact, what I've gone through has made me a much stronger person." She laughed softly. "'Stubbornly resilient' as my best friend, Erica, is fond of telling me."

He wanted to ask her why she wasn't angry with the Lord instead of being so accepting. How could she smile when all he wanted to do was grit his teeth at all the injustices he'd suffered?

"And the other reason I understand what Katie is going through," she continued, "is because I'm legally blind."

# Chapter Five

*Blind?*

Nathan watched Alyssa go, his feet frozen in place. Her admission ringing in his ears. How was that possible? He would have known if she was visually impaired. Wouldn't he? His mind played back their first meeting. Alyssa hadn't seen Katie charging toward her until it was too late. And then when he'd joked about his daughter being a bull in the china shop, Alyssa's expression had grown troubled. She'd told him she'd been looking for The Toy Box, which, of course, she'd been standing right in front of. And it would make sense as to why her friend had driven her to Braxton, leaving Alyssa without any means of transportation for what could amount to several weeks. She couldn't drive.

He had so many questions he wanted to ask Alyssa about her unexpected revelation, but he would wait until they had some modicum of privacy. He loved his daughter dearly, but Katie was like a little mynah bird and there might be things Alyssa would prefer his daughter not announce to all and sundry.

"Daddy!" His daughter's voice carried down the hallway, no doubt from the cafeteria where she'd gone to give Alyssa McCall a tour.

He forced his feet to move in that direction, once more stopping just inside the open doorway. Leaning against the unfinished door frame, he casually crossed one booted foot over the other, planted his thumbs into the front pockets of his jeans, and watched as his daughter did the job her uncle had given her to do.

"This is where the tables are gonna go," she told Alyssa with a wave of her arm.

"I can see them there already," Alyssa replied with a nod.

"You can? How?" Katie looked around, a bit bewildered by the statement.

Alyssa laughed softly. "Like this." Her long lashes shut against cheeks lightly dusted with freckles like Katie's. "Close your eyes."

His daughter did as she was told. "All I see is dark."

"The dark is your mind's eye."

"I have three eyes?"

More of Alyssa's soft laughter filled the air.

"Not exactly. Think of the darkness you see as an empty chalkboard. Imagine the room as you'd like to see it and create it on your blackboard."

"Mine has round tables," she chirped excitedly.

"The best kind. Now add some color to the walls."

"What color?" Katie asked, her eyes squeezed tight.

"Whatever color you'd like," Alyssa told her. "Make it polka-dotted if it pleases you."

"Polka dots?" Nathan cut in, drawing both their gazes his way. "We're building a rec center, not doing some fancy home makeover show."

"Your daughter is designing her own version of what she imagines this room should look like," Alyssa explained, with admirable patience. "You'll be happy to know, however, that polka dots are not part of my plans for this room."

"That's a relief," he muttered.

"I'm leaning more toward painting a line of dancing carrots across the back wall."

His brow shot up. "Dancing carrots?"

"To promote healthy eating," she said, attempting to muffle a snort of laughter.

She was teasing him. Two could play that game. "Might wanna throw in a couple of juicy, red apples to remind folks that an apple a day keeps the doctor away."

"Daddy," his daughter groaned, her eyes once again closed. "I'm trying to draw and all your talking is making me mess up."

At his daughter's admonishment, a smile tugged at Alyssa's mouth, the sight of which distracted him thoroughly. He shouldn't be noticing her smile. He should be focused on the work he had to do. But how could he not notice it with her standing so close? Truth was, he hadn't even looked twice at another woman since Isabel's passing. Why now? Why her?

"You ladies go ahead and work on your drawings," he told them. "I need to go see how things are coming along with the indoor pool." His gaze shifted back to Alyssa. Thick lashes lowered once again, she returned to the game she was playing with his daughter. The gentle smile on her pretty face had his own mouth pulling upward.

He flattened his mouth as soon as he realized what he had done. He wasn't supposed to be thinking of someone he was going to be working with in that way. Then again, other than Isabel he'd only ever worked with men. Straightening, he pushed away from the door frame and slipped out into the hallway, trying to clear the image of Alyssa McCall's bright smile from his mind.

He strode toward the room that held the yet-to-be-filled Olympic-sized swimming pool. Alyssa McCall might get under his skin in an unwanted way, but he couldn't deny the positive effect she had on his daughter. He just hoped Katie wouldn't become too attached, seeing as how Alyssa was only there until the project was finished. And if things progressed the way he hoped they would, her stay in Braxton would be even shorter than planned.

"Something wrong, big brother?" Carter asked the second Nathan entered the swimming pool room.

"No," he replied. "Why?"

"The grimace you had on your face when you came in had me wondering," his brother replied as he slid the handle of the hammer he'd been holding into the oversize loop at the side of his tool belt.

"That wasn't a grimace," he said with a frown as he walked around to do a visual inspection of the tile work that had just been laid along the top inside edge of the pool walls. He wasn't getting into what was bothering him with his brother. He preferred to work things out on his own. "I just have a lot on my mind right now."

"Ah, so that would explain why you forgot

to mention that Miss McCall was both young and pretty," his brother said as he accompanied him around the pool. "Wait until Logan catches a glimpse of her."

He shot his brother a scowl. "Alyssa is off-limits to Logan and the rest of the crew. And would you mind keeping your voice down? Sound carries in this place, remember?"

"Off-limits, huh?" his brother repeated with an all-too-knowing grin as he continued on around the pool ahead of Nathan. "That include you?"

"Don't make me take a staple gun to your big mouth," he warned as he knelt to inspect a section of the tile where a little more grout needed to be added.

Carter chuckled, not the least bit intimidated by Nathan's empty threats. "Thought so," he murmured as he moved from window to window along the far wall, inspecting their crew's work.

Nathan's frown deepened. He wasn't looking for a replacement for Isabel. Katie and Carter were going to have to accept that. Just because Carter had managed to push aside everything they'd been through to find happiness with Audra didn't mean that was what he and Logan wanted.

"Good to see you're giving my question some

real thought. Definitely a step in the right direction." Carter walked away, making his way back around the pool to the door.

Nathan's gaze drilled into his brother's departing form. "I hardly know the woman," he called after him. That was the best he could come up with? What happened to "mind your own business, Carter" or "don't you have a life of your own to pay mind to?"

Before he could change his response, Alyssa stepped into the room.

"Don't tell me your tour guide gave you the slip," Carter said with a smile.

She laughed. "No. Katie sent me in here to wait while she ran to the water fountain for a drink. Truth be told, your niece is an excellent tour giver."

"Trained her myself," he boasted with a grin.

Nathan found himself waiting for her gaze to shift to where he still knelt on the far side of the pool. Waiting to be on the receiving end of one of those smiles she so freely seemed to give.

"Don't believe a word he says," Nathan called out when her attention failed to shift in his direction. "He's always trying to take credit for everything that goes right."

"Nathan?" Alyssa's gaze searched the far side of the room. For him.

How could he have forgotten? She couldn't

see him from where she stood. Up close she seemed to do better. Or was she that good at making herself fit in? Just as he did when it came to church. Sure, he went every Sunday. But he never prayed. Not anymore. Not since the Lord had seen fit to take Isabel away in the prime of her life. He only went for his daughter's sake. Isabel had wanted their daughter to be strong in her faith. He would see her wishes carried through. Even if going to church tended to be an emotional challenge for him.

"Over here," he replied as he got to his feet, his voice echoing in the vast room. "Far right corner."

Carter chuckled. "I doubt she needs directions, big brother. You're standing right here in the same room."

Even from where he stood, Nathan could see the unease move through Alyssa. But it wasn't his place to tell Carter why he'd made his whereabouts known.

"I didn't realize you were in here," she confessed, looking Nathan's way.

Carter's expression slid from playfully grinning to utterly and thoroughly confused. "I seem to be missing something here."

"We can talk about it later," Nathan told him. Once he'd had a chance to discuss things with Alyssa. He needed to know just how much she wanted others to know about what she'd admitted to him.

"It's all right," she said, sending him that smile he'd been hoping for. "It was foolish of me to think no one would find out."

"Find out what?" Carter inquired, his gaze shifting back and forth between the two of them.

"I didn't realize your brother was standing on the other side of the room," she admitted, "because I'm visually impaired." She bit into her bottom lip as if expecting some sort of negative response from his brother.

Was that how the world reacted to her disability? Had she had her feelings hurt by others because of it? The thought of anyone being intentionally cruel to Alyssa had him clenching his fists.

His gaze shifted to Carter, who studied Alyssa closely. No doubt trying to read the sincerity in her words. A habit that came from having a younger brother who was always trying to pull the wool over their eyes. But unlike Logan, Alyssa wasn't playing around and Nathan knew the moment his brother recognized it for the truth it was.

Carter nodded, offering her an accepting smile. "Reckon that'll spare you from seeing my brother's ugly mug on a daily basis."

Nathan stiffened. What could his brother

have been thinking making a remark like that? Couldn't he tell how uncomfortable Alyssa had been just admitting… Before he could finish the thought, her sweet laughter filled the air.

"I'm not *completely* blind," Alyssa clarified as she reined in her laughter. "Just enough for doctors to give me the life-altering label of legally blind. That being the case, I'm fully aware that your brother's mug is nowhere near as bad as you're trying to make me believe it is."

Carter looked his way, one lone, dark brow raised.

*She'd noticed his face*, Nathan thought with a hint of satisfaction he shouldn't be feeling. But it was hard not to appreciate the compliment. Especially when it served to put his brother in his place for his teasing remarks.

"I've gotta admit I had no idea," Carter said, shaking his head. "So do you wear corrective contacts?"

"Carter," Nathan grumbled as he finally walked around the pool to join them.

"I don't mind answering," she assured him, turning her attention back to his brother. "I don't wear contacts, because the problem isn't with my eyes. They're perfect. This issue is with the part of my brain responsible for processing the images my eyes see. The result of head trauma

I suffered in a car accident a few years ago. It won't get any worse, but it's not reparable either."

Carter frowned. "I'm real sorry to hear that."

"Before you let my visual impairment worry you, know this. I'm very good at what I do. I have a degree. I have several years of hands-on experience. I can still get an accurate layout of the places I'm designing for and then am able to give the customer what it is they are looking for."

"You don't have to sell yourself to me," Carter cut in, beating Nathan to it. "You were sent here to do the job by a highly respectable interior design firm. You're giving up your personal time over the holidays to stay here and help see our project through to completion. That tells me all I need to know." His brother looked Nathan's way. "You got any issues with her doing this job?"

He met her gaze from where she stood just a few feet away. "I'd be lying if I said I didn't have any issues with it. At least, at first. Not because of her visual limitations, but because of my own emotional ones."

Surprise lit his brother's face at the heartfelt admission. Understandably so. He wasn't a man who openly admitted his vulnerability. But when Alyssa had so openly shared hers, he felt the pressing need to join her.

Nathan went on before he lost the nerve. "I

seem to have a problem letting go of the past. I know that. And Miss McCall—"

"Alyssa," she reminded him, her tone kind.

"Alyssa," he repeated, unable to take his gaze off the comforting smile she aimed his way, "understands my reasons for it and, I hope, knows that I'm gonna work on turning my mind-set around."

Her smile lifted even higher. "Not an easy task, but it can be done. I'm living proof that we can wish things could be the way they were, but still accept God's will."

Nathan's jaw clenched, despite the smile pasted on his face. He was just about to voice his opinion on God's will when his brother cut him off.

"My wife's been craving dill pickle spears with a side of chocolate milk!"

The blurted-out words had both him and Alyssa casting questioning glances in Carter's direction.

His brother shrugged with a grin. "Figured since everyone else was doing it, I ought to make a confession, too."

No, what his brother had been doing was attempting to avoid a debate over being so accepting of God's will, knowing where Nathan's feelings lay in that regard. It worked. It was hard to focus on his anger toward God when his brother was discussing dill pickles and chocolate milk.

Nathan rolled his eyes. "That's not a confession."

Laughing once again, Alyssa nodded in agreement. "Not even close."

"How about if I find myself craving it, too?"

"I'm thinking that's one confession you ought to have kept to yourself," he told his brother. Just as he would his stirring interest in Alyssa's pretty smile. Because his focus needed to be on completing this project on time.


"You looked like you could use a Big Dog's double-thick double-chocolate shake."

Alyssa glanced up from the notes she'd been making on her laptop to find the waitress who had served her lunch holding a lidded cup out to her with a friendly smile.

"It's the perfect fix for anything that's troubling you." She nodded toward the open laptop.

Alyssa sat back with a sigh. "That obvious, huh?"

"Only a little," the young woman replied, her kind smile widening. "And only to a waitress who prides herself on having the ability to know when her customers are in need of something."

She looked up at the other woman. "You know, a chocolate shake is exactly what I need to clear my head. I seem to be having trouble focusing on my work at the moment." Her thoughts were too preoccupied with what she'd learned that day about Nathan Cooper and his precious little girl.

"Well, I hope it helps. I can't imagine how hard it must be to leave your own life for weeks to work in a town where you don't know anyone," the young woman added. "Speaking of which, consider that milk shake a token of my appreciation for offering your services to our town's effort to rebuild what we lost in the tornado."

Her kind words touched Alyssa. "Thank you," she said, taking the offered cup. "I'm happy to be even a small part of it all. But how did you know who I was?"

"Word travels fast in a small town. I'm just sorry I didn't know who you were when you were here the other day or I would've thanked you then." She held out her hand. "I'm Lizzie Parker. Waitress by day. Student by night. Takes one to pay for the other."

Accepting the offered hand, Alyssa said, "Alyssa McCall. Been there. Done that. I worked my way through college, too. What are you studying?"

"Meteorology."

"Admirable field. You must be really good with math and science."

"Fortunately, I am." Pushing her long, strawberry blonde ponytail back over her shoulder, she sighed. "But that doesn't keep me from wondering sometimes if I'll ever get my degree. I'm twenty-four and not even halfway through with my course work."

"You'll get there," Alyssa assured her. "You just have to keep your eye on the goal."

Lizzie laughed softly. "You and Nathan should work well together. That's the very same advice he gave me."

Alyssa certainly hoped they would. Their working relationship hadn't exactly started off on a positive note. Only now she understood why Nathan had reacted to the news of her working with him on the project the way he had. Leaning in, she took a sip of the shake and moaned softly. "He and I seem to have the same opinion of the shakes here, as well. This truly is the best shake I've ever had."

"Nathan should know," Lizzie said with a smile. "Katie drags him in here nearly every week to get one. Not that he complains. That man has a sweet tooth to match his daughter's."

Alyssa's thoughts went back to her conversation with Doris and Myrna. It appeared that men, even big, rough and tough men like Nathan Cooper, had a thing for sweets. Growing up without a father and having dated very little left her embarrassingly ignorant of these little tidbits of information.

"I had better let you get back to work."

Alyssa's gaze shifted to the notes she'd been making on her laptop and then back up at Lizzie. "Maybe we can talk again sometime."

"I'd like that. I miss having the chance for girl talk. Most of my close friends went off to college and moved to other parts of the country."

Alyssa could relate. She was already missing Erica, even though her best friend was only a phone call away. Reaching into her purse, she pulled out a business card, handing it to Lizzie. "My number's on here. Call me when you have some free time and we can meet up. I'd love to know more about the town and the people who live here."

Lizzie eyed the card and then slid it down into the front pocket of her apron. "I look forward to it." Just then an elderly couple stepped inside the restaurant. "Back to work," she said with a grin. "Let me know if I can get you anything else."

"I think I'm good," Alyssa said. "Thanks again."

With a nod, Lizzie hurried off to greet the

couple. Smiling, Alyssa sipped at her shake. Maybe her stay in Braxton wouldn't be quite as solitary as she'd feared it might be.

# Chapter Six

Katie sprang out into the hallway of the rec center as Nathan was passing by. As usual, she was all smiles and sunshine, which had his own smile widening.

"Daddy, guess what!" she exclaimed as she raced toward him. His daughter never did anything at an unhurried pace. At times, he fretted over it, concerned she would reinjure her leg. But her doctor had assured him that she could do almost anything other children her age did, so he fought the instinct to tell her to slow down.

"What?" he replied as he caught her up in his arms, spinning them both in a slow circle.

"I decorated the new art room all in my head," she answered with a happy giggle.

He loved seeing his daughter so enthusiastic about life. There had been a time shortly after Isabel's death that he'd feared she'd never know joy again. But his baby girl was made of tough stock. She'd grieved the loss of her mother and grandparents, and then like a hardy little wild-flower she'd bloomed again.

"You did?" he said, easing her down until her tiny feet rested on the cement floor. "Keep that up and I might just have to hire you on to work for Uncle Carter and me."

"And Alyssa."

"*Miss* McCall," he corrected.

"It's all right," Alyssa said as she joined them in the hallway, notebook in hand. "I asked Katie to call me by my first name."

"'Cause we're friends and that's what friends do," his daughter explained with a bright smile. "Alyssa said I could help her decorate the rec center while I'm here."

His gaze shifted. "She did, did she?" As glad as he was to see his daughter so happy, he couldn't help but be concerned that Katie was forming an attachment that was going to leave her heartbroken once Alyssa went back home to San Antonio.

Alyssa nodded. "We were going through some of the paint color strips I picked up at the hardware store this morning and I have to say her choice of both the main and the accent colors was spot on." She smiled down at Katie. "Your daughter has a real knack for artistic design."

Something else she'd inherited from her mother, he thought with a sad smile. "I know," he replied, his gaze fixed on his little girl. "We have a wall at home that displays my daughter's artistic ability." He ruffled Katie's hair playfully.

"Daddy," she groaned. "I was only three when I did that. Why can't we paint over it?"

"Because your mother loved it." Lingering grief edged his voice.

"Little Miss Katydid," Carter said as he stepped into the hallway from the lobby. "Look who came to see you."

"Uncle Logan!" she shrieked.

Logan knelt, arms extended. "I was outside working on the landscaping and decided I needed to come inside and get myself a Katie fix," he told her as she wrapped her arms around his neck in a loving embrace. His gaze moved past the head of dark curls beneath his chin to settle on Alyssa. "I heard a rumor there were two pretty girls hanging around this place, but it's plain to see some rumors sell the truth short. You two are beyond pretty."

A faint blush moved across Alyssa's cheeks.

Pressing a kiss to Katie's brow, he eased from her hold and straightened, extending his hand to Alyssa. "Logan Cooper."

She slid her hand into Nathan's brother's with a warm smile. "Alyssa McCall."

"Pleasure to meet you," his brother replied with a crooked grin. "A real pleasure."

"Don't you have some more trees to plant?" Nathan grumbled.

"Nope," Logan replied, holding on to Alyssa's hand longer than necessary. "All planted."

"It was nice to meet you," Alyssa said, retrieving her hand from his brother's eager grasp. "I hate to run off, but I need to take another run through the swimming pool room and finish up my notes."

"Mind if I—"

"I'll go with you," Nathan said, cutting off Logan's offer of joining her for the walkthrough.

Carter snorted, muttering something under his breath about being glad he was already hitched. Then he scooped Katie up, draping her over his shoulder like a sack of potatoes. "Katydid and I are gonna take a run into town to the hardware store to pick up some flooring samples for Miss McCall to look over tonight."

"But I got work to do," Katie proclaimed.

"This is work," his brother assured her. "As Miss McCall's helper, it's your duty to see she has the supplies she needs to do her job. And she's gonna need to choose the flooring right quick so we can get it ordered and put down as soon as the painting is done."

"Reckon I best go," Katie agreed, looking up at her uncle. "You might pick out the wrong thing."

"My thoughts exactly," Carter teased. Then he turned to Logan. "You wanna ride along?"

"Thanks, but I've gotta run by the nursery to talk to Jack. I'm gonna need a few more flats of pansies and white and purple violets."

Jack Dillan owned the local nursery Logan used for his landscaping company. He was also the father of the only woman his youngest brother had ever truly loved. Hope Dillan. Even though they'd only been teenagers at the time, Nathan had believed the two would eventually marry. But he'd been wrong, and his brother had spent the past nine years putting on a happy front when both he and Carter knew it to be a cover for the deep hurt that lingered just below the surface.

"Send him our regards," Nathan said.

"Will do."

"You might wanna take a look at some of those Virginia pines Jack's got in the back field while you're there," Carter suggested. "We're gonna be needing one for the rec center's Christmas party."

Logan nodded. "I'll be sure to do that."

"I wanna help pick it out!" Katie exclaimed. "Can I please, Uncle Logan?"

He chuckled. "I promise to let you help me when it comes time to chop one down. And after the holidays, we'll turn it into mulch and add it to the landscaping outside." Logan turned to Alyssa. "You free for dinner? I could pick you up after work. Maybe show you around town."

"She's already got plans." Nathan scowled as he answered for her.

"I do?" Alyssa couldn't keep the surprise from her voice.

Nathan's gaze stayed fixed on his younger brother. "She's having dinner with me and Katie tonight."

"She is?" Katie squawked excitedly from her perch atop Carter's broad shoulder.

A grin slid across Logan's face as he turned to Carter. "You're right."

Carter nodded. "Told you so."

Logan nodded with a chuckle, then tipped his cowboy hat to Alyssa. "Pleasure meeting you." He looked to Carter. "Walk me out?"

Their brother nodded. "Right behind you."

Alyssa watched them go, Katie's giggles trailing behind them as they disappeared from sight.

"You have any brothers?" Nathan asked.

She turned to him. "No. I was an only child."

"Consider yourself lucky," he said, shaking his head.

"Oh, I don't know," she said. "I think having brothers like yours would have made my life so much more interesting."

He chuckled. "That's because you haven't spent any real stretch of time with them." Then he inclined his head. "Come on. I'll walk with you to the swimming pool room."

"I like your brothers," she admitted as they moved down the hallway.

"I do, too," he agreed. "At least, most of the time."

They stepped into the oversize room that housed the Olympic-sized swimming pool. Alyssa opened her notebook and slid the pen free of the spiral binding. "What would you think of my going with a rich, warm sand color on the walls with a twelve inch strip of dark blue going around the room at chair-rail height? I was thinking about hand painting small sections of waves in a bright white paint inside the blue accent stripe."

His gaze scanned the room as if envisioning her plans. Then he nodded. "I like it." He glanced her way. "But it's a big room. That's a lot of wave painting."

"I don't mind. I'd rather work than sit around doing nothing."

He nodded in understanding. "I feel the same way. We've got painters who can take care of the basic painting of the walls. Just give me a list of what colors go where."

"Will do."

"My men can paint walls, but adding decorative murals or designs will have to fall to you."

"Perfect." She started around the pool only to have him join her.

"Watch your step," he said, placing himself between her and the still-empty pool.

She smiled up at him as they walked. "Have you always been so protective of others?"

He looked away, falling silent.

What had she said? "Nathan?"

He heaved a heavy sigh. "I wasn't there for my wife when the storm hit. I should've been there to protect her."

Reaching out, she placed a hand on his arm. "She wouldn't blame you for that."

He stopped, turning to face her. "But I do."

Her heart went out to him. For all he'd gone through. For the undeserved guilt he'd taken upon himself. For the pain she saw in his eyes. She gave his arm a gentle squeeze before letting her hand fall away. "It was a tornado. They're sudden and unpredictable. You had no way of knowing. If you had, you would have moved

Heaven and earth to be there for her and for Katie. Your wife knew that."

His expression changed. Softened. "Do you always know the right thing to say?"

"Hardly," she said with a smile. "I just have a tendency to be honest and speak from the heart."

"You say that as if it's a bad thing."

"It can be," she admitted softly. "When people find out about my condition…" Her words trailed off.

"It shouldn't make a difference."

"But it does," she said, looking up into caring blue eyes. "I'm a realist. I've simply had to learn how to work around the prejudices and hold strong to the belief that God has a plan for me."

"You're a remarkable woman, Alyssa McCall," he told her with a smile that bordered on tender.

They stood unmoving for several long moments before Alyssa forced her gaze away from his handsome face. "I should let you get back to work," she said, trying to focus on the notes she'd been making in her notebook.

"You sure you're okay in here?"

She glanced up at him. "I'm fine. Though I do appreciate your concern."

He nodded. "Um…about dinner tonight…"

She looked up at him questioningly. "Dinner?"

"When I told my brother you already had

plans, I was sorta putting the cart before the horse. Would you like to join Katie and me for dinner this evening?"

Other than being invited over to Erica's for family dinners, she'd never had anyone offer to make dinner for her. "I'd love to."

His smile widened. "How do you feel about creamed chicken and biscuits?"

"It's one of my favorites."

"Katie's, too," he admitted. "She likes to help me make it. But I have to warn you. The biscuits are gonna come from a can."

She laughed softly. "Is there any other kind?"

Before he had a chance to respond, his cell rang. "Excuse me," he said, pulling his phone from the front pocket of his jeans. "Nathan Cooper speaking."

Alyssa stepped away, to give him some privacy for his call.

"Millie," he said, his deep voice echoing in the open room. "How's your sister doing? Sorry to hear that." There was a long pause before he said, "Take all the time you need. I'll figure things out with Katie."

Alyssa didn't mean to eavesdrop, but the large, empty room amplified everything. "Everything okay?" she asked when he disconnected the call and stepped over to join her.

"The woman who usually takes care of Katie

for me while I'm at work had to go to Laredo for a family emergency. Apparently Millie's sister has had some complications following surgery, so she's gonna have to stay out there with her longer than expected."

"Is her sister gonna be okay?"

He nodded. "Thankfully, yes."

"That's why you've been bringing Katie into work with you?" she asked. At least he had for the two days Alyssa had been working at the rec center.

"I don't really have a backup," he said with a frown. "My brother's wife, Audra, just found out she's expecting and is having a rough time of it with morning sickness and all. I didn't feel right asking her to watch Katie for me. Not when she's already got two little ones of her own to watch over."

"Understandable. And Katie seems to love coming here."

"You've made her feel very special, allowing her to help you out. I want you to know that I really appreciate it."

"I don't mind. I enjoy spending time with her."

"But when you told her she could help you with the interior design plans, you had no idea Katie would be coming to work with me every day now that she's on Christmas break. Possibly until this project is done. I intend to make sure my daughter understands that she's not to make a pest of herself."

"Please don't," she implored. "I want her to feel free to ask questions and offer suggestions."

"Even if those suggestions entail dancing carrots?" he asked with a chuckle.

"The dancing carrots were my idea," she reminded him with a smile. "But, yes, even then. I love helping children discover their creative abilities."

"Fine. I'll hold off on having a talk with my daughter. But if she gets to be too much, I want your promise that you'll let me know."

"You have it," she said warmly.

He glanced toward the door and then back down at her. "I'll be in the women's locker room if you need me."

"Excuse me?"

He chuckled again, a sound she found herself being drawn to more and more. It was warm and soothing and had her own smile widening. "We're installing the wall lockers today."

"Oh, of course." She walked him to the open doorway. "What time should I be at your house tonight?"

"Katie and I will drop you off at the boardinghouse after work and then come back for you around six. Does that work?"

"Yes, but I—"

"Can walk," he finished for her. "I think we've already established that you've got a thing for walking. Even in the cold. But my momma raised us boys to be gentlemen. That means picking up a lady we've invited to dinner. Not having her find her own way there." That said, he stepped from the room, leaving Alyssa watching after him.

His momma sounded like a wonderfully caring woman. But then it only stood to reason, considering the kind of men she'd raised. And that night she'd be having dinner with one of them. A man who had become both father and mother to his young daughter after the tragic loss of his wife. One whose love for that little girl shone so brightly it couldn't be missed whenever they were together. A man who worked hard.

And if all of that didn't make Nathan Cooper special in her eyes, he was the first man since her accident that hadn't been put off by her visual impairment. He'd not only accepted her for who she was, he trusted in her ability to do the job she was there for. That meant the world to her because she had to succeed in the job she'd been sent there to do. Doing so, she prayed, would help convince her firm that she truly was capable of more than they were allocating to her. And before that could happen, she would have to prove to Nathan and his brothers that she was capable of the task she'd been given. Their feedback could make or break her career as far as Pure Perfection Designs was concerned. She could not fail.

He had his brother to blame for his temporary insanity. If Logan hadn't come into the rec center all smiles and charm and asked Alyssa out, he would never have blurted out that she already had plans—with him.

He'd done it to protect her. His little brother was a fun-loving flirt who didn't have any intentions of settling down. While Logan would never deliberately set out to hurt Alyssa, his brother didn't know what she'd gone through. Yep, that was why he'd done what he'd done.

*Son, a half-truth's the same as an untruth.* He could almost hear his momma speaking those words. And she'd be right. If he were being completely honest with himself, he'd admit that he'd cut his brother off at the pass because *he* wanted to be the one to take Alyssa to dinner. Or, as was the case, invite her over for dinner. He wanted to get to know more about her. Wanted to spend time with her outside of work.

A wave of guilt swept over him. He shouldn't be wanting anything. It felt like a betrayal of what he'd had with Isabel. His focus needed to be on finishing the rec center, not on a ten-derhearted female who would be gone in a few short weeks.

"Is it time yet?" Katie hollered from where she stood looking out the front window, shoes and coat already on.

His gaze shifted to the clock on the kitchen wall. Ten minutes to six. "It's time," he acknowledged with a frown.

"Yay!" his daughter exclaimed, racing for the door. "Hurry up, Daddy!"

Turning off the burner, Nathan moved the pan of creamed chicken to the back of the stove top and dropped the lid onto it to keep it warm. Then he grabbed his coat from the back of the kitchen chair, shoving his arms into the sleeves as he followed his daughter outside.

"You know Miss McCall will be leaving in a few weeks, maybe less," he told his daughter as he leaned over to buckle her into her seat. Something he appeared to need reminding of himself.

"Not if she likes it here," Katie countered. "Then maybe she'll stay."

"She has a life somewhere else, Cupcake." Settling back against the driver's seat, he fastened his seat belt and started the engine. "A job. Friends. A place of her own." He pulled out and started down the gravel road.

"But if I had some mistletoe, I'd have a new mommy and she'd have you."

His daughter was persistent if anything. "Alyssa is a very special lady. And as nice as she is, chances are she already has someone special in her life. Now no more talk about her staying here in Braxton. Just enjoy the time we have to spend with her while she's here." How did he make his daughter understand that he was incapable of loving another woman ever again? That his heart had broken irreparably when he'd lost Isabel.

A tiny frown of disappointment pulled at his daughter's lips as she replied with a sigh, "Okay, Daddy."

Her response left him feeling both relieved and guilty, the second an emotion he seemed to be experiencing more of the past few days.

Katie, as resilient as a Texas Tea Bush, turned her attention to the bag of crayons and paper she'd brought with her from home, her "work" supplies, and began singing softly to herself as she sifted through the various colored crayons in the box.

A few minutes later, they pulled up in front of the boardinghouse. His daughter sprang from the truck and raced for the house before Nathan could call her back. Shaking his head, he let himself out and strode toward the deep-set traditional porch with its assortment of antique rockers. His daughter had already disappeared inside by the time he reached it, no doubt eager to see the kittens before returning home.

The front screen door swung open just as he started up the steps and Alyssa stepped outside. The sight of her nearly had him stopping mid-step. Instead of the jeans and sweater she had worn when working today, she was wearing a simple knee-length floral dress with a short-waisted jean jacket. Only there was nothing simple about it. The pale peach flowers with their dark green leaves complemented the golden highlights of her red-gold hair. His gaze slid down to the fawn-colored boots she wore.

"Hello."

Her voice drew his gaze upward. Her smile caught and held it. "Hello," he replied, feeling oddly off-balance.

"Doris took Katie back to the kitchen to see Bluebell, Rhett and Scarlett, who are busy feasting on a plate of tuna. Would you like to come in?"

He shook his head. "We'd best get going. I've got dinner waiting on the stove. Would you mind just giving Katie a holler?"

"Sure thing," she said. "Be right back."

The second she slipped back inside, he pulled out his cell and dialed his brother.

Carter answered on the second ring. "What's up, big brother?"

"I need you to come over for dinner."

"When?" his brother asked.

"Tonight," he replied. "In five minutes."

"You want me to come over for dinner in *five* minutes?"

"Bring Audra and the kids, of course. We should be home by then."

"We?"

"Alyssa, Katie and me."

"Why?"

Because he didn't trust himself where Alyssa was concerned. He didn't want to notice she was pretty. Didn't want to sit across the table from that beautiful smile and yearn for it to be aimed at him. But he settled for "Because that's what family does. They get together and have dinner."

"Maybe so, but I'm afraid that won't be happening tonight," Carter said. "Audra just took the kids upstairs for their baths. Besides, we already ate."

"You could come. You don't have to eat."

His brother laughed. "If I didn't know better, I'd think you were afraid to be alone with Alyssa."

"She's wearing a dress," Nathan said with a frown.

"As women sometimes do," Carter pointed out with another chuckle, enjoying Nathan's discomfort a little too much. "Besides, you'll have Katie there to keep you from drooling too much."

Why had he ever thought calling Carter was a good idea?

Alyssa's gaze swept over the wraparound porch that made up the front and one side of Nathan Cooper's house. Unfortunately, it was one of those times when her vision wasn't at its best, so she couldn't make out much more than the shape of the porch and the color of the house—white trimmed in a steel blue.

"Farmhouse?" she asked, knowing Nathan would understand.

"Yes, but not an old one," he explained. "I built it the year before Katie was born."

"What I wouldn't give to have a porch even half this size at the town house I live in," she admitted.

He shrugged. "A porch is a porch."

But it was so much more than that. It was a place for family and friends to sit and share special moments. A place for couples to watch the stars from at night. A place it suddenly struck her that neither of them could enjoy to its fullest. Because she didn't have family to share those special moments with. And Nathan had lost the woman he loved.

The screen door creaked open and Katie popped her head out. "Are you guys coming?"

"On our way." Nathan reached for the door and then, holding it open, motioned her inside.

The house was clean with very little clutter she noted as he walked her through the spacious living room, which was open to a large dining room area. She tried to make out the pictures on the walls, but the images in them were nothing more than darkened blurs. Were there pictures of Isabel hanging there? Something told her the woman had been quite beautiful. And perfect. A wife without flaws.

Why did it matter? It wasn't as if this was a date. It was simply Nathan and Katie being kind. She forced her gaze down to the table in front of her and the floral-edged china that had been set out for the meal. "The table looks lovely."

"Katie insisted we bring out the good china," Nathan said. "The plastic silverware was her idea, as well," he added with a grin.

"My favorite kind of silverware," Alyssa replied, appreciating the effort Katie had put into making dinner special.

Katie beamed at Alyssa's approval of her hostessing skills. "It's good on picnics, too."

"I'll bet it would be."

Nathan chuckled. "You make it sound as though you've never used plastic silverware when you've gone on picnics. They must do things a bit more fancified in San Antonio than they do here."

She kept her gaze fixed on the table. "I don't know how they do it in San Antonio or anywhere else. I've never been on a picnic."

"Ever?" Katie gasped.

She shook her head, forcing her gaze upward. "Afraid not."

"Not even when you were little?"

"Katie," Nathan said, his tone gentle. "Not everyone goes on picnics."

"They should," she insisted. "Can we have an inside picnic, Daddy? Like we do sometimes when it rains?"

"I doubt Miss McCall wants to eat her dinner on the living room floor."

Katie looked up at her. "Do you wanna have a picnic with us?"

Alyssa exchanged glances with Nathan, whose expression was nothing less than apologetic. She smiled, then looked down at Katie. "I would love to have a picnic with you and your daddy. Do I need to watch out for ants?"

Katie giggled. "No, silly. Ants live in the grass. We're gonna be sitting on the rug in front of the fireplace."

"Well, then," she said, feeling nearly as excited as Katie was, "do you have paper plates? I'd hate to use your father's good china on the floor."

"We'll use the china," Nathan said as he moved past her to collect the dinner plates and salad bowls from the table. "Alyssa, would you mind grabbing the silverware? Katie, you're in charge of finding us a blanket to have our picnic on."

His daughter raced off to fetch it.

"I'm sorry this isn't gonna be the dinner you expected," he said over his shoulder the moment Katie was gone.

"No," she agreed. "It's not. It's gonna be even better."

He turned to face her. "You really don't mind?"

She shook her head. "Not at all." Her gaze fell to the dishes he held. "I just feel bad you have to go through all this trouble because of me. The table looked so nice."

He shrugged. "It's no trouble. Besides, my daughter's right. Everyone should experience a picnic at least once in their life. Or as close to a real picnic as we can offer," he added with a grin, "seeing as how it's too cold outside to have one out in the yard."

*Don't cry*, she told herself as the sting of tears in her eyes threatened to have her doing just that. No one had ever done anything so special for her. Ever. Embarrassed by her inability to control her emotions, Alyssa kept her back to him as she gathered up the plastic silverware. A tear slid down her cheek and she closed her eyes, willing the rest not to fall.

"Alyssa?" Nathan's caring voice wrapped around her. "You okay?"

"Fine," she said, her voice breaking.

"Are you crying?"

"One tear doesn't constitute crying," she assured him, her lips trembling as she turned to face him with a reassuring smile.

"Was it something I said?" he asked with a worried frown.

"Yes," she answered honestly. "But not in a bad way."

"How can my making you cry not be a bad thing?" Confusion lit his blue eyes.

"I've never had anyone do this for me," she said, waving her hand over the stack of delicate china he held in his large, work-roughened hands. "Make dinner for me. Invite me on a picnic."

Understanding filled his eyes and his mouth quirked up on one side. "An inside picnic."

"I know," she said with a soft sniffle. "Don't mind me. I'm just being silly."

"Not at all," he said. "I'm glad that I…that is, Katie and I could give you this. It's the least we could do for all you are doing for our town."

"Katie is so lucky to have a father like you," she said softly. "So kind and caring. So strong in your love for your family and in your faith—"

"Got it!" Katie exclaimed as she dashed back into the room, carrying a faded blue blanket.

Thankfully, Katie's return saved Alyssa from saying any more. She stepped away from Nathan to help Katie spread the blanket out before the fireplace.

Nathan joined them, the three of them working together to set their new table.

Alyssa glanced up to find him watching her, the amber glow of the fireplace lighting his smiling face. She smiled back, wishing there were more men like Nathan Cooper in the world. But experience had shown her his kind was a rare find.

"If you two can finish setting up for our picnic," Nathan said, "I'll head into the kitchen and warm up the biscuits so we can eat." His tall form straightened until he towered over them as they knelt on the blanket. "Can I fix you ladies something to drink while I'm in there?"

"I made lemonade," Katie announced with a proud tilt of her tiny chin. "With real lemons."

"Lemonade sounds like the perfect drink for a picnic," Alyssa said excitedly, making Katie's smile widen even more.

"Two lemonades coming right up." Turning, Nathan disappeared into the kitchen.

Katie settled cross-legged onto the blanket. "Do you like my tree?" she asked, pointing to the small, spindly tree standing next to the fireplace. One probably no taller than Katie herself.

Alyssa took in the hazy glow of the miniature white Christmas lights. Tilting her head slightly to bring the sparsely decorated tree into better focus amid the shadowy spots that hampered her vision that evening, she took in the smattering of colorful bulbs that hung from several of the slender branches. A garland made of popcorn wound its way around the tree, while a piece of burlap snugly surrounded its base. It reminded her of the tree in *A Charlie Brown Christmas*.

"It's the perfect size," she told Katie.

"I picked it out myself," she said with a glance toward the kitchen. "Daddy cut it down for me."

"Where will your big tree go?" she asked, looking around.

"We won't have one. Daddy says he's not good at decorating," she explained. "But I think it's 'cause he's too busy."

Her heart went out to Katie, knowing what it felt like to spend Christmas in a home void of holiday spirit. Only in Katie's case it wasn't because her daddy didn't care. It was because he was a single father, trying to run a company while raising a young daughter. He was probably too tired after a long day's work to feel like stringing up Christmas lights or putting out holiday decorations. Maybe she could help. After all, decorating for the holidays was a favorite pastime of hers. And she'd love nothing more than to give Katie the sort of Christmas she had always longed for as a little girl.

# Chapter Seven

"I have to admit I was surprised to see Alyssa arrive with you and Katie this morning," Carter said as he and Nathan stood watching Alyssa and Audra talking outside of Braxton's only church.

"Katie invited her to join us today," Nathan grumbled. Going to church always left him feeling torn. There was a part of him that used to believe in God's good grace, in what it meant to have unyielding faith. He supposed that part of him still lingered somewhere deep inside, having been a part of him since childhood. But he'd long since locked that part of himself away.

Besides, if they hadn't given Alyssa a ride there, she would have walked. Doris and Myrna, though devout Christians, almost never left their boardinghouse. After Doris's husband passed away, she'd developed an aversion to going out, and Myrna chose to remain at her sister's side. They even had their groceries delivered. He understood the urge to lock yourself away after losing someone you love, but he didn't have that option. Not with Katie in his life. He simply carried on.

"She's wearing a dress," his brother said with a chuckle, distracting Nathan from his troubled thoughts. "Is that why you're in a mood?"

She was. A long, almost to her ankles, light blue dress that fluttered in the breeze. Covered by the fitted, camel-colored jacket she wore. He looked Carter's way with a scowl. "Worry about your own wife's dress."

Carter chuckled. "Just trying to figure out why you're acting like you got a burr stuck in your britches, and I remembered how her wearing a dress to dinner last week had you all in a fluster."

"It doesn't have anything to do with her dress," he said. Even if she did look right pretty in them.

His brother grew more serious. "Care to let me in on what's really eating at you? You haven't been yourself for days."

Nathan's frown deepened as he glanced Alyssa's way again. "I'm not the man she believes me to be."

"How so?"

His gaze shifted, locking with his brother's. "She's a good woman."

"You won't get any argument from me there."

"Honest."

His brother nodded. "A definite plus."

"I've never known a woman stronger in her faith."

His brother studied him with a critical eye. "Okay. I've got all that. What I'm trying to figure out is how her having all those positive qualities fits in with her not knowing who you really are."

*So strong in your love for your family and in your faith.* Her words had stuck with him, forcing him to take a look at the man he'd become. A man lost. A man pretending to be something he wasn't. A man undeserving of someone like Alyssa but failing in his attempts to fight the pull she seemed to have on him.

Nathan sighed deeply, his gaze settling on his booted feet. "Alyssa thinks that because I'm a good father and take Katie to church every Sunday, I'm a man who's strong in his faith."

"And you're not?"

He looked to his brother. "You know I'm not."

"I know your faith has been tested," his brother replied matter-of-factly. "And that you're angry with God. But I also know that you'll find your way back. Just as I did."

Could he? He wasn't so sure. Nathan's gaze was drawn in the direction of the church. Alyssa, with her beautiful smile, was laughing at something Audra had said. Sunlight glinted off her hair and lit her face. It felt like that same sun was seeping into his chest, warming him. But he knew it wasn't the sun melting the part of his heart that had been frozen for two years. It was Alyssa. And he found himself wanting to be a better man. The man she thought him to be. The man he once was. Problem was, wanting to do so and being able to do so were two vastly different things.

"Frowning like that isn't the best way to win a woman over," Logan said as he joined his brothers where they were standing at the edge of the church's parking lot, waiting patiently while the women visited and the children played. "Females tend to prefer warm, friendly smiles," he said, directing his words toward Nathan. "I could show you how it's done if you like."

"Not the best time to poke fun at him," Carter warned. "Big brother here's got himself all tied up in knots."

Logan's gaze shifted back to Nathan and he sobered instantly. "You really like her," he said, the surprise clear on his tanned face.

Not that Nathan could blame him. He and Logan had held firm to their decision to remain confirmed bachelors. Or at least they both had until now.

"He *really* likes her," Carter said, answering for him.

"I never said that," Nathan said, his attention drawn once again to the woman he'd made cry—in a good way.

His brother snorted. "As if you had to. It's as plain as the longing we see written on your face. You like her, but you're determined not to."

"I loved my wife."

"We all did," Logan said.

"But she's gone," Carter said as if Nathan needed to be reminded of that fact. "It's been two years. No one is gonna think badly of you for wanting to find happiness again."

His jaw clenched as emotion roiled in his gut. "I can't."

"You can," Logan countered. "Isabel would have wanted you to be happy again."

The about-face his youngest brother had just done had Nathan's tossing a questioning glance his way.

"Don't go looking at me like that," Logan grumbled. "I know what we decided, but you have Katie to think about."

Carter nodded.

"It doesn't matter how I feel," he told them. "Alyssa's only here for a couple more weeks before she returns to her life in San Antonio. The best thing I can do for my daughter—and for Alyssa—is to remember that."

"Nathan…" Carter said, his tone pleading.

He held up a hand. "No. For the next couple of weeks, I'm gonna focus on getting the rec center done, which means keeping things between Alyssa and me strictly professional. Nothing more."

"Can't you do both?"

"My attention has to be directed toward seeing that the dedication to those lost in the storm happens as planned. I can't afford to be sidetracked."

"Nathan—"

"Uncle Nathan!" Audra's seven-year-old son, Mason, hollered out as he and Katie raced out to the parking lot, putting an end to his brothers' determined attempt to convince him otherwise.

He cast a smile their way. Mason and his baby sister, Lily, had been abandoned by their birth father, Audra's ex-husband, both emotionally and physically. How any man could do that to his child was beyond Nathan. However, Carter was in the process of legally adopting them. They already considered him their father, just as his brother considered them every bit as much his children as the baby Audra now carried inside her.

"Daddy, guess what!" Katie exclaimed as she did her best to keep up with her cousin in spite of her slight limp.

"What?" he asked with a grin as they came to a stop in front of him, their little cheeks pink from their sprint across the churchyard.

"You're gonna help Miss McCall with the manger," Mason told him.

"I'm what?" he said, looking in Alyssa's direction.

She mouthed *I'm sorry* before turning her attention back to whatever it was Audra had been saying to Reverend Johns' wife, Rachel, and several other women who had gathered around them.

*Sorry about what?* His gaze dropping back down to the two smiling children in front of him, he said, "What are you two talking about?"

"Mrs. Gillis was asking if anyone had time to help work on the manger," Mason explained.

"Alyssa said she'd be happy to," Katie said excitedly. "I told Mrs. Gillis that you'd be happy to help, too, 'cause you're a team. And you have to drive her here."

"Looks like someone's gonna have to focus on more than just the rec center," Logan said with a grin.

Carter snorted.

Nathan growled, then immediately regretted

doing so. Thirty-year-old men did not growl. Especially with two children standing within hearing range.

"I'm not doing it alone," he told his brothers. "You two are volunteering, too."

"Think he needs us there to keep his focus where it ought to be?" Logan asked Carter with a grin.

His brother nodded. "Might be a good idea. He won't be much help if he's constantly hammering his thumb instead of the nails he's supposed to be pounding in."

Audra and her five-year-old daughter, Lily, came over to join them before Nathan could defend himself.

"Darlin'," Carter greeted her with a loving smile. Then he reached out, curling his arm around his wife's slightly expanded waist. "Enjoy your visit with Alyssa?"

"Very much so," she answered with a smile. "She's so easy to talk to. I feel like I've known her forever."

Nathan understood what Audra meant about Alyssa being so easy to talk to. She had a way of making people feel at ease around her. He nodded in agreement.

"I'm looking forward to spending more time with her," his sister-in-law said. "We're going to get together for some girl time with Lizzie one of these days. Mrs. Johns offered to watch the children for a few hours so we could."

"Sounds like fun," Carter agreed, despite his happy expression drooping ever-so-lightly. "But you have me to watch the children. Why would you need the reverend's wife to help out?"

Her expression grew tender. "Because as much as I love it when you spend time with my—" she caught herself, her warm smile deepening "—*our* children, you have a very important job to get done. You never know how late you're going to be working. Especially during the next couple of weeks. So I was grateful for Rachel's kind offer. Unfortunately, Alyssa won't be in town for much longer, so we can't wait until after the rec center is finished."

At the mention of Alyssa's imminent departure from Braxton, Nathan's searching gaze moved once more in the direction of the church's front walkway. Those who had milled about after that morning's service were now gone. Alyssa included. Had she forgotten something, and gone back inside to fetch it? No, he definitely recalled her holding her purse when they'd walked out. Maybe she'd gone around to the other side of the church to see where the nativity scene would be set up.

"If you're looking for Alyssa," his sister-in-law said behind him, "she asked me to let you know that since it's such a beautiful day, she's going to walk back to the boardinghouse."

While the day was pleasantly warm, despite it being a week into December, it was still a long walk. And she would be doing it in heels. "Katie, get in the truck," he said, his gaze now fixed in the direction Alyssa was headed.

"Why don't you leave Katie with us?" Carter suggested, drawing Nathan's attention his way. "The kids have been wanting to have some real playtime together with their new cousin."

Audra nodded. "Katie can stay for dinner and you can pick her up later this evening."

"Please, Daddy!" his daughter implored, working him over with her big brown eyes.

He hesitated only a moment before giving his consent. "Mind your manners."

"I will!"

He watched as she scampered off to Carter's truck with an equally excited Mason and Lily.

"Katie will be fine," Audra assured him before she and Carter took their leave.

"You best get a move on or Alyssa will be at the boardinghouse before you even start your truck."

He turned to find Logan watching him with a knowing grin.

"Traitor," Nathan grumbled as he started for his truck.

"Call it a change of heart," his brother called out. "At least where your remaining a bachelor is concerned."

Nathan yanked open his truck door and slid into the cab. One of these days, his little brother was gonna get what was coming to him. Hopefully in the form of a female who made Logan every bit as unsettled as Alyssa made him.

*Unsettled* didn't even come close to describing how he felt after he'd driven all the way to the boardinghouse only to be told by Myrna that Alyssa hadn't gotten home yet. How was that possible?

Unease moved through him as he pulled away from the boardinghouse. Had Alyssa gotten lost? Or had she stopped somewhere in town to pick something up before heading back.

A flash of baby blue through the trees where the walking bridge crossed over the Blue Falls Creek caught his eye. Pulling off the road, he cut the engine and jumped out of the truck.

Taking the dirt path through the woods, he stepped from the trees to see Alyssa standing on the narrow bridge. Relief swept through him at finding her safe and sound.

Her head was tipped back, her eyes closed, every inch of her awash in sunlight. A gentle breeze had the hem of her dress fluttering lazily around her legs. She looked right pretty standing there, taking in the sweet sounds of nature, feeling the warm caress of sun on her face, the whisper of the wind.

All of those things he hadn't allowed himself to fully appreciate for so long. But Alyssa had a way of making him feel things. Even when he fought hard not to. Carter had once told him he needed to come back to the land of the living. Those words came rushing back to him now as he moved toward the bridge. That was exactly how he felt. Alive.

The sound of a twigs cracking under quickened footsteps had Alyssa turning.

"There you are."

"Nathan," she breathed, her heart thumping. "You startled me."

"Reckon that makes us even then," he drawled as he moved to stand beside her on the narrow wooden bridge. "I went looking for you when I left church and you were nowhere to be found. I was afraid… Well, I thought maybe you had gotten lost."

Her first thought was to inform him that she was perfectly capable of taking care of herself. But the fact that he cared enough to worry about her well-being had her apologizing instead.

"I was on my way back to the boardinghouse when I heard the rippling of the creek beyond the trees. I couldn't resist taking a few minutes to appreciate it." She looked up into his handsome face, concern and something more filling those deep blue eyes. "I never meant to worry you. I asked Audra to let you know that I was gonna be walking back to the boardinghouse."

"She passed your message on," he said with a frown. "What I don't understand is why you didn't wait for Katie and me to give you a ride home."

Turning, she looked out over the rail, her gaze fixed on the gently flowing water below. "You were busy with your family and I didn't wanna take you away from that." It sounded better than *Because you've shown me what my life's been missing and being around you and your wonderful family only makes me want more.*

"Alyssa," he said, "if I made you feel like you weren't welcome to join us…"

The last thing she wanted was for him to feel as though he'd done something wrong. She lifted her gaze to his. "You didn't do anything."

"Then it was something someone else said?" he asked with a frown.

"No," she answered honestly. "Everyone has been more than welcoming. It's just that I'm used to watching others with their families, not partaking in it." With the exception of Erica's family. But even then she only saw them all together a few times a year.

"Then it appears we'll have to work on that," he said, his words tender. "You don't have to be family to take part in our conversations."

"Thank you," she said, lowering her gaze. "I'll keep that in mind."

"You do that. It appears I'm not the only one in my family who enjoys your company," he added with a grin.

She looked up at him in surprise. "I thought you were counting down the days before you were rid of me."

His expression grew serious. "In the beginning, yes. But it didn't take long before I realized what a positive addition you were— are—to the team."

"Tell that to my employers," she mumbled. "They don't think I'm capable of doing my job any longer."

"They'd be dead wrong," he said firmly. "But that's not why I want you to stick around. Truth is, I like having you around, and I know for a fact my daughter does, as well. At the risk of crossing some unspoken professional line, I'd really like to get to know you better. Outside of work."

Her eyes widened in surprise. "You wanna spend personal time with me?"

His devastatingly handsome smile returned. "I'd like the opportunity. Why do you seem so surprised?"

"Because…" What if Nathan found her lacking as other men had? The thought he might be disappointed kept her silent.

"Alyssa…" he prodded gently.

She sighed deeply. "Because I'm not perfect."

"And you think I am?" he replied with a husky laugh. "Far from it," he admitted. "Just ask my brothers."

That made her smile. "You know what I mean. There are things I can't do because of my vision."

"There are plenty of things I can't do and I have twenty-twenty vision."

"It's not that simple," she said, wanting him to know the full extent of what he was getting into.

"Nothing in life is simple," he told her. "I've learned that the hard way." Turning, he clasped his hands atop the railing. "When Isabel died, I forgot how to breathe. How to feel. I put on a brave face for my daughter, but inside I was numb." He glanced her way. "And then you came into our life. I can't explain it, but when I'm around you, I feel like I can breathe again."

Unshed tears stung her eyes. "That's the nicest thing anyone's ever said to me," she said, her words catching on a choked sob.

"All I'm asking for is a chance to get to know the woman you are beneath the hard-working, incredibly focused interior designer I see at work every day. The woman who was so deeply touched by something as simple as a picnic on my living room floor. A chance to become… friends."

Emotion clogged her throat. "I'd really enjoy spending more time with you and Katie outside of work." Nathan Cooper truly was a man worth holding on to. If only as a good friend. He hadn't run the other way the moment he'd learned she was legally blind. Yet she knew better than to expect anything more than the friendship he spoke of, despite the comfort she felt working alongside him at the rec center and sitting beside him and Katie in church.

His smile widened. "Are you in a hurry to get back to the boardinghouse?" She didn't miss the hint of eagerness in his voice.

"No," she said, wondering what he could be up to. "Why?"

"There's something I'd like to show you." His gaze dropped down to the sling-back heels she'd worn to church, and his mouth twisted into a thoughtful frown. "Reckon I'm gonna have to carry you there."

"Carry me?" she said, letting out a little shriek as Nathan scooped her up in his arms.

"Can't have you twisting an ankle," he said as he carried her across the bridge to the other side, and then onto another wooded trail that ran along the curving creek bed.

"Just how far are you gonna carry me?" Not that he showed the least bit of strain at having to do so. The man was incredibly strong, both inside and out.

He grinned down at her as they moved along the well-worn trail. "I'd carry you all the way to the boardinghouse if the situation called for it. But the waterfall is only about another hundred feet or so ahead."

"Waterfall?"

"Not a large one," he was quick to explain. "But it's right pretty, nestled in a vee of rocks where it cascades down into the creek below."

He seemed so excited that she didn't have the heart to tell him she probably wouldn't be able to see the beauty of what he was describing. It was the thought that counted. And that he'd thought to share something so beautiful with her touched Alyssa deeply.

The trail opened up onto a small grassy bank, beyond which was a wider expanse of the creek and what, though blurred, appeared to be a rocky hillside. Nathan set her on her feet and then said in a hushed voice, "Shh…just listen."

She heard birds chirping happily in the trees

above them. The creek gurgling a few feet away from where they stood. And the sweetest sound of all, the rhythmic fall of water into the creek below. Like a gentle rain, but centered in one place.

It suddenly struck her that Nathan hadn't brought her there to *see* the waterfall. He'd taken her there to *hear* it. At that moment, she felt like the luckiest woman in the world.

"It's beautiful," she said, her words tight with emotion. "Thank you for bringing me here."

"Maybe you can come back to Braxton for a visit this summer when the creek is warmer and we can wade in to see the falls close up."

"I would love that," she said, looking up at him. "Katie, too?"

His smile widened, seemingly pleased by her question. "And Katie, too."

"Nathan had you over for dinner?" Erica gasped on the other end of the line. "Are we talking about Nathan the incredibly hunky construction worker you've been working with on the rec center? The one who wasn't exactly thrilled to have you there?"

Alyssa smiled. "One and the same."

"So am I to assume he's gotten over any issues he had about working with you?"

"He has." She went on to tell Erica all about

the special picnic she'd shared with Nathan and Katie that past week and how he'd taken her to church with them. "That was so incredibly sweet of them to take you on a picnic," her friend said. "And then to invite you to go with them to church, I know that had to mean a lot to you."

"It did," Alyssa admitted. To find a man who valued faith as much as she did meant the world to her. And then what he'd done for her at the waterfall. She grew misty-eyed just thinking about it. "And there's more."

"The man already sounds perfect. What more could there be?"

"He told me that he'd like to see me outside of work."

Another gasp. "As in dating?"

"As in building a friendship," she clarified.

"Some of the best relationships have begun with friendship."

She couldn't bring herself to get her hopes up. "I don't think Nathan's looking for that kind of relationship. But I'm willing to take things one day at a time and see where things go between us."

"Don't even think about it!" her friend blurted out, her words followed by the phone clattering on the other end of the line.

Alyssa blinked. She certainly hadn't expected

that reaction from her friend. Erica had been trying to convince her that her Mr. Right was out there. And now that she found a man who came close to being her image of Mr. Right, her friend was demanding she not let it happen?

"But I really like him."

The sound at the other end of the line was muffled. Alyssa stepped over to her bedroom window at the boardinghouse, hoping it might improve the connection, which had suddenly gone from good to bad.

She was just about to hang up and call Erica back when her friend came back on the line.

"Sorry about that. I was in my closet hanging up some of Michael's shirts and my darling daughter decided to use our bed as a trampoline. I dropped my cell into the laundry basket on my mad dash out of the closet to grab her."

Relief swept through her. "So you weren't speaking to me when you said 'Don't you dare'?"

Her friend laughed. "Are you kidding me? I am beyond thrilled for you. There's no one I know more deserving of finding true happiness. And if your friendship with Nathan leads to more? Well, then I'll be more than happy for you."

"I know you would be." Alyssa glanced toward the clock on the nightstand. "I hate to cut our call short, but I need to head downstairs. Myrna and Doris fixed Texas chili and homemade cornbread for dinner."

"Then I'd better let you go. Munchkin here is due for her bath anyway," her friend said. "Aren't you, munchkin?" Whatever Erica did elicited squeals from her daughter. "Have fun, Alyssa."

"You, too." Alyssa disconnected the call, a smile stretched wide across her face. Maybe, just maybe, her friendship with Nathan would lead to more, and she would have her very own happily-ever-after someday, too.

## Chapter Eight

"You have no idea how excited I am for our girls' night out," Lizzie announced as Alyssa slid into the backseat of Audra's minivan. "Monday was crazy busy at work. Thankfully today was a little slower. But then I only work half days on Tuesdays unless Verna needs me to stay on longer."

"You aren't the only one looking forward to tonight," Audra said from the front seat. "By the time my third child arrives, there won't be anyone willing to watch that many kids all at once."

"If I lived around here, I'd be more than happy to help you out," Alyssa told her, meaning every word of it. Audra's children were adorable and well mannered.

Lizzie sighed. "If I didn't have a full schedule with work and school, I'd volunteer, as well."

"It's not as if I mind spending most of my

time with my children. They truly are blessings from God. As is my supportive and loving husband."

Alyssa smiled, but inside she ached for all those things. To be a mother. A wife. Loved. Shaking the dismal thoughts away, she said cheerily, "So where are we going?"

"Ryan's Pies and Pins," Lizzie replied excitedly. She had volunteered to choose their entertainment for that evening and Alyssa and Audra had happily agreed. "I reserved us a lane. We can enjoy some of Ryan's hand-tossed pizza while we bowl a few games."

"Bowling?" Alyssa said worriedly.

The two women looked her way.

"If you'd rather not bowl," Lizzie said, "we can do something else. I should have asked if the two of you liked bowling before making definite plans."

"It's not that." Alyssa wasted no time assuring her. "I actually love bowling. Although I haven't done so since…"

"Since?" Audra pressed worriedly.

Alyssa sighed. They would have figured it out sooner or later anyway. "I'm visually impaired. Legally blind is the actual medical diagnosis I've been given."

"I had no idea," Lizzie gasped.

"Alyssa," Audra breathed.

"It's all right," she told them, pasting on a bright smile. "Most people don't know. A few years ago, I was involved in a serious car accident. By God's grace I survived, but the head trauma I suffered left me visually impaired."

"I'm so sorry," Audra said.

"Don't be," she told her. "God gave me a second chance at life. I refuse to waste one precious moment of it feeling sorry for myself. Instead, I wanna live as normal a life as I possibly can. And that includes bowling with my two new friends."

"Then that's exactly what you'll do," Lizzie announced, her youthful smile returning.

A few minutes later, they were walking through the entrance of the bowling alley and pizzeria.

"There's a single step down about five feet in front of you," Audra announced as she closed the door behind them.

"Thanks for the warning," Alyssa said with a grateful smile. She might not have noticed in the dimly lit entryway. Thankfully the much larger bowling alley area farther inside was abundantly lit.

"Well, well, if it isn't my long-lost little Lizzie Parker," a man with wavy blond hair and a neatly trimmed goatee greeted from behind the counter when they stepped into the bowling area.

She approached him. "We have a lane reserved for six thirty."

"I know you do," he said, his charming smile widening. "Saw your name on the book when I came in." His gaze slid to Audra and he nodded. "Mrs. Cooper."

"Audra, please."

His attention shifted to Alyssa and he let out a low whistle. "The pretty ladies in this town just keep on multiplying."

Lizzie rolled her eyes with a groan. "Reckon I should've warned you both before we got here that Ryan fancies himself a bit of a smooth-talking ladies' man."

He chuckled. "Can't change something that's a pure fact." The ladies rattled off their shoe sizes to Ryan and he pulled three pairs out from under the counter. "Here you go. You ladies are on lane eighteen. Can I get you anything else?"

"A menu please," Alyssa said.

"Thank you," Lizzie said as he held one out to her. "And for the record, I'm not little and I haven't been lost. Just busy with work and school. If you'd ever stop by Big Dog's, you'd have known that."

"And give my competition the business?" he said with a teasing grin.

Alyssa took in the playful banter between the bowling alley owner and Lizzie, and couldn't help but wonder if there was something more going on between them. Not that it was any of her business if there was. Turning her focus elsewhere, she listened to the sound of bowling balls being dropped onto the wooden lanes before rolling down the alleys. In the distance, she heard the crack of pins. The familiar sounds took her back to a more carefree time in her life. Oh, how she had missed this.

"Okay, spill," Carter said as Nathan drove them to the bowling alley across town.

"Spill what?" Nathan said.

"What's got you so out to sorts that you've called us all together for an evening out," his brother replied.

Nathan frowned. "Does something have to be wrong for me to wanna spend time with my brothers outside of work?"

"Yep," Logan muttered. "Something's definitely troubling him."

Nathan released a long-drawn-out sigh. "It's nothing."

Logan leaned forward from the backseat of Nathan's truck. "Nothing, as in Alyssa?"

"I asked her to be friends," he said with a

frown as he turned into the parking lot outside of Ryan's Pies and Pins.

Logan laughed. "As opposed to being her enemy?"

Parking in one of the empty spaces, Nathan turned to glower at his brother.

"Logan's right," Carter said. "So you asked Alyssa to be friends. Why do you think that's such a bad thing? We happen to like her."

So did he, Nathan thought with a frown. More than he ought to.

Carter clapped a hand atop Nathan's shoulder. "What do you say we go get our game on? Loser springs for the pizza."

"I'm in," Logan said. "Prepare to buy me dinner, boys."

Win or lose, it didn't matter to Nathan. He needed this night out. A night where his thoughts could be centered on something other than his pretty coworker, Alyssa McCall.

No sooner had they stepped into the place than soft laughter caught Nathan's attention. Sure enough, the very woman he'd gone to the bowling alley to escape thinking about for one evening was laughing with his sister-in-law and Lizzie at the far end of the bowling alley over a ball Audra had just rolled.

His gaze snapped to Carter. "Did you know they would be here?"

His brother shook his head. "Nope. I don't think Audra knew where they were going tonight. Lizzie was in charge of planning tonight's festivities."

His brother frowned as he stared across the room at his wife. "Do you think she ought to be lifting that ball in her condition?"

Logan shrugged. "I'm no expert, but I've seen pregnant women picking up their other children with no problem. They've gotta weigh more than a bowling ball."

Nathan's attention was centered on Alyssa, his brothers' conversation becoming nothing more than a hum of chatter behind him. The girls were clearly enjoying their night out. He watched in surprise as Alyssa stepped up to take a turn. He worried over her twisting an ankle in the gutter if she misjudged where she needed to be standing.

Logan stepped up beside him, giving him a nudge. "You wanna go somewhere else?"

Nathan shook his head, his gaze fixed on Alyssa. "She's bowling," he stated worriedly.

"And doing quite well," Carter stated. "She just took down nine pins."

"Well, well, this must be family night."

They turned to see Ryan, a smile lighting his face.

"Appears that way," Logan agreed.

Ryan extended his hand, greeting each one of them. He and Logan had gone to school together and still managed to get together on occasion in spite of their demanding businesses.

"Carter?"

All heads pivoted toward the sound of Audra's voice.

"Hey, darlin'," he greeted with a loving smile.

Her smile wavered, concern lighting her eyes. "Are the children all right?"

He looked confused for a moment before promptly setting her mind at ease. "Right as rain and in good hands with the reverend and his wife."

"Then why are you here?" she asked, looking every bit as confused as his brother had been moments before.

"I invited him," Nathan told her.

Carter nodded. "We had no idea you'd be here."

"Didn't you see the minivan outside?"

Actually they hadn't, Nathan thought. They'd all been too distracted by his moment of emotional panic. "We can go somewhere else," he suggested.

She laughed. "Why ever would you do that?

Come join us." She looked to Ryan. "Is the lane next to ours reserved?"

He shook his head. "It's all yours if you want it."

"I don't think—" Carter began only to have Nathan cut him off.

"We'll take it."

"Are the children okay?" Alyssa asked when Audra returned alone.

"They're fine," she said, her relief evident. "The men decided to enjoy a night of bowling after work and had no idea we'd be here. I hope you don't mind, but I invited them to join us."

"The more the merrier," Lizzie chirped.

"I don't mind," Alyssa said. She welcomed any chance to spend time with Nathan and build on their growing friendship.

"Something told me you wouldn't have an issue with it," Audra teased, her words making Alyssa blush. "As soon as Ryan can find shoes large enough to fit their big feet, they'll be right over."

A few minutes later, three big strapping men moved toward them. Alyssa's gaze was drawn immediately to Nathan.

"Ladies," they greeted in unison as they walked over to place their balls in the ball return tray.

Nathan turned to face her with a smile. "Fancy meeting you here."

She returned his smile. "Where's Katie?"

"The reverend and his wife are babysitting," he answered with a smile. "The kids are working on decorations for the rec center's Christmas party."

"Sounds like fun."

"Speaking of fun," Lizzie said with a cheery smile. "Why don't we share the lanes and keep all the scores on one sheet?"

"I'm not so sure that's a good idea," Nathan told her. "We Coopers tend to get very competitive."

"So do I," Alyssa countered with a playful smile. "But if you men are afraid you might be outbowled by us women…"

"It's not that," he said worriedly.

"If you're afraid her vision's going to hold her back," Audra said, guessing the cause of his hesitation, "think again."

Lizzie nodded in agreement.

Nathan's dark brow lifted in surprise. "They know?"

Alyssa smiled, her gaze moving to the two women who had befriended her. "Friends should always be honest with each other."

"What do you say we get this game on the

road?" Logan announced. "I'm starving and loser buys the pizza tonight."

"We'll play for pizza another time," Nathan told his brother with a frown.

"Why?" Alyssa asked. "I'm game if the other girls are."

"I'm in," Audra said.

Lizzie dropped down onto the scorekeeper's chair. "Me, too."

"Alyssa," Nathan said worriedly.

"Don't you dare count me out, Nathan Cooper."

A slow smile moved across his handsome face. "I'd never count you out. You forget, I've seen firsthand what you're capable of once you've set your mind to something."

Alyssa smiled at the compliment. Things were going well with the rec center. Both Nathan and Carter were supportive of her ideas and suggestions, even making a few of their own.

"Well, now that we have that settled, you two are up," Lizzie announced as she began adding names to the electronic scoring screen.

Without a moment's hesitation, Alyssa stepped up to the tray of bowling balls and reached for the one she'd chosen to bowl with that night.

Nathan joined her. "I was surprised to find you here. But I'm glad I did."

She smiled up at him. "I'm gonna remind you of that after the final scores are tallied."

An amused grin moved across his face and a dark brow lifted. "Someone counting their chickens before they're hatched?"

"Maybe," she said with a giggle, and then she started over to her lane. "Oh, and, Nathan…"

"Yes?"

"I may have forgotten to mention that I was captain of my college bowling team for two years straight. Division champs both times."

"Watch out, Nathan," Carter called out, "I think she's their ringer."

He gave a husky chuckle. "I think you might be right."

She adored this playful, easygoing side of him. He'd been working himself so hard to get the rec center done that it was nice to see him taking some time for himself.

"How about I bowl left-handed instead?" she suggested with a grin as she lifted her ball.

"You're ambidextrous, aren't you?"

She giggled. "Maybe."

With a groan, he said, "Something tells me dinner's gonna be on me tonight."

This could be her life. Sharing special moments with Nathan, no matter how silly they might be. Working with him. Laughing with him. Loving him. *Loving.* She pushed that thought away. Nathan wanted to be friends. Nothing more. She couldn't allow wishful thinking to make her believe otherwise.

At the end of the evening, Alyssa and Nathan sat at the bottom of the score rankings with only one throw remaining for each of them. "Looks like one of us is buying," he said as they reached for their balls.

"Hope you brought your wallet," she said with more confidence than she felt. Bowling wasn't nearly as easy as it had been when she had perfect vision. But she'd had fun anyway.

It was Nathan's turn so he stepped forward in the lane. Then, with perfect form, he sent the ball spiraling toward the pins, then sent the pins scattering.

"A split," Lizzie announced, no doubt for Alyssa's benefit for which she was extremely grateful. All evening the others had found ways to let her know where things stood without making her feel like she was a hindrance to their game.

"Go ahead," he told Alyssa.

"You might as well finish first," she told him.

"Alrighty," he said, reaching for the ball that had just shot up the ball return. Wasting no time, Nathan walked over, aimed and threw.

"Field goals only count as a score in football," Carter said with a husky laugh.

"Bummer," Logan snickered.

Nathan motioned for her to go. "Your turn."

She needed at least seven pins to beat him. In college, that would have been a done deal. Tonight, however, odds weren't in her favor. But she'd give it the old college try. Easing her ball up into the air in front of her, she prepared to send it spiraling down the lane.

"Hey, darlin'," Nathan called out the second she drew back to roll the ball down the aisle.

The weighted ball slipped from her grasp and onto the floor with a loud *kerthunk*, rolling at what could only be described as a turtle's pace up the long alley. She spun around to face her handsome opponent with a disapproving frown. "What?"

"I was gonna offer to fetch you a lighter ball if you thought the one you're using was too weighty," he said with feigned innocence. "Reckon it doesn't matter now."

"You distracted me on purpose!"

Grinning, he shrugged. "What can I say? A man will do almost anything to save his pride from taking a complete thrashing."

"Nathan Cooper, you're a cheater!"

"He is that," Logan agreed from the bench.

"Just goes to prove that the saying 'cheaters never win' is true," Carter remarked from where he sat on the bench, arm curled around his wife. He motioned in the direction her ball had gone.

Nathan turned, a deep sigh passing through his parted lips. "Serves me right, I suppose."

"What are you talking about?" Alyssa said as she followed their gazes.

"You just rolled a strike," Lizzie told her.

"I did?" she gasped.

"You did," Nathan confirmed. "Roll again, darlin', while I dig my wallet out. Looks like I'll be buying tonight."

"That's the most fun I've had in a long time," Lizzie exclaimed as they pulled out of the bowling alley's parking lot.

"Me, too," Alyssa said, smiling.

"Despite losing and having to buy pizza for everyone tonight, something tells me Nathan enjoyed himself even more than we did," Audra said. "Then again, we know why that is."

Alyssa knew they were referring to her. "Nathan and I are just friends." And if she told herself that enough times, maybe she'd be able to accept it.

"I don't know," Lizzie said. "Sure felt like more than that to me. Every time he looked at you, his expression softened. I don't ever remember him smiling as much as he did tonight."

"Alyssa wasn't the only one holding a man's attention this evening," Audra said with a grin.

Lizzie looked to her questioningly. "Someone was watching me?"

"Logan?" Alyssa guessed. Not that she'd noticed, but then she'd been slightly distracted by another Cooper brother.

"Nope," Audra said.

"Then who…" Lizzie began and then stopped. "Please tell me you are not referring to *him*."

"Him who?" Alyssa blurted out.

"Ryan," both women replied. Only Lizzie's response was far less enthusiastic.

Alyssa smiled. So she wasn't the only one who'd noticed something in the air between them. "He seems very nice."

Lizzie snorted. "He's the most frustrating man ever born. 'Little Lizzie,'" she said, repeating his earlier remark. "The man is determined to think of me as his little sister's childhood playmate instead of the woman I've become. Not that it matters anyway. I'm no longer the young girl who followed him around like some lovesick puppy. I've grown up. And in doing so, I've come to accept that life doesn't always go the way we'd like it to."

Alyssa nodded. "I understand completely."

"Oh, Alyssa," Lizzie gasped. "I'm so sorry. Here I am rattling off my frustrations when they're so minor compared to what you and Audra have been through."

She offered a reassuring smile. "We've all been through things in our lives we'd rather not have had to go through. But here we are today, stronger women because of it. God is good."

Lizzie nodded. "So true."

"Amen," Audra said as she pulled up in front of the old farmhouse where Lizzie lived with her elderly parents.

"Thanks again for such a fun evening," Lizzie said as she gathered up her purse. Reaching out, she opened the sliding door and stepped from the minivan.

"Maybe we can do it again sometime," Audra said hopefully.

"I would like that. Night, girls." Closing the door, Lizzie stepped away from the van, waving as they pulled away.

Alyssa waved back, wishing with all her heart she could be there to join them for another girls' night out, but she would be returning to San Antonio as soon as her work there was done, leaving behind her new friends, dear sweet Katie and the man who was quickly stealing her heart. Lizzie had the right of it. Life didn't always go the way one hoped it would.

# Chapter Nine

"Thank you so much for agreeing to help us out this evening," Reverend Johns said as he and Nathan carried more lumber around the side of the church to where the nativity scene was being set up next to a large, sprawling oak. "I know you already have a lot on your plate."

"Glad to lend a hand," Nathan replied. A part of him hoped that giving something back to the church would ease some of the guilt he felt every Sunday when he sat determinedly tuning out whatever sermon the reverend was giving to the congregation. There had been a time he used to soak up those sermons and leave feeling good about his life. But since losing Isabel and his parents, all he felt was empty. Until his daughter had invited Alyssa to join them for church the Sunday prior. That morning had changed something inside him.

Alyssa's presence beside him in church had soothed him, giving him a feeling of peace he hadn't known for a very long time. And, much to his surprise, he found himself really listening to the reverend's sermon. He had spoken of forgiveness. Would he ever be able to do that? Let the anger and resentment he felt toward God wash away and start his relationship with the Lord anew?

He caught sight of Alyssa as they rounded the corner of the church. She sat alone at the folding table that had been set up a short distance away from where the manger was being constructed. Her head was bent, her focus solely on painting wood cutouts Carter had made of sheep both standing and lying down that would be staked into the grass near the manger. The sight of her hard at work made him smile. Alyssa dedicated herself fully to any project she committed herself to. He admired that in her.

After depositing the two-by-fours onto the stack by the manger, he walked over to see the one woman he couldn't seem to get off his mind.

He stepped up behind her, taking in the perfectly detailed sheep drying atop the table. She was good. "Is there anything you can't do well?" he asked with a grin.

Her head lifted, the brush stilling in her hand as she glanced back over her shoulder at him.

A sweet smile moved over her pretty face. "A few things."

"Somehow I find that hard to believe," he teased. "I've yet to see it."

Setting the paint brush down, she turned in the chair to look up at him. "For starters, you probably wouldn't want me driving around in your truck."

The playful smile she had on her face while talking about something that had to be painful for her made him admire her all the more.

"And," she continued, her smile edging up even higher, "I think I'd hesitate just a bit before asking me to operate a chain saw."

Laughter rumbled in his chest and then spilled out. "I'll keep that in mind," he said, paying no mind to the looks the sound of his laughter had drawn their way. His attention was centered on her. A living, breathing ray of sunshine.

She glanced past him toward the partially built nativity scene. "How are things going?"

He followed her gaze. "We're moving right along. Carter should be back soon with the plywood for the roofing and Logan's picking up straw to spread out across the roof and over the stable floor."

"I know your helping out here this evening wasn't exactly your choice."

Her apologetic tone drew his gaze back to

her pretty, fretting face. No, it hadn't been his choice. If he'd had his way, he would have steered clear of the whole thing. But now that he was there, he was grateful Katie had volunteered his services. It felt good to be a part of this again.

"How could I not be here? We're a team, remember?" he told her with a grin, repeating Katie's description of his and Alyssa's relationship.

Her smile returned. One that had proved infectious with his little girl.

More often than not since losing her mother and her grandparents, Katie had been withdrawn and quiet around anyone not close to her. But since Alyssa's arrival, there had been a change in Katie. An inner spark that came out in a constant deluge of bright smiles, excitement and laughter. Alyssa had somehow managed to bring his daughter out of her emotional shell, something even the therapist he'd taken Katie to after the tornado hadn't been able to do.

Forcing himself back from his wandering thoughts, he said, "I should let you get back to painting."

"I suppose," she said with an exaggerated sigh. "These sheep won't paint themselves."

"And the stable won't build itself either," he agreed. "I'd best get back over there."

"Will you be able to finish it tonight?"

"The framing will be done," he replied. "After that, the ladies of the church will take over, adding the finishing touches."

"I wish I could be here to see everything all put together."

"Why wouldn't you be?"

She looked his way. "At the rate things are going here, the rec center will be finished before Christmas Eve and I'll be back in San Antonio."

"Then stay."

"What?"

"Stay here in Braxton, Alyssa. At least through the holidays like you planned. For Katie," he said, and then he added, "And for me."

She opened her mouth to tell him she couldn't, but nothing came out. How could she refuse him? She didn't want to leave, despite knowing she had to. But there was no reason she couldn't stay on a few extra days. It would give them more time to see what might develop between them. And they'd be together for Christmas. Excitement filled her at that thought. While she would miss visiting with Erica and her family, she would be spending the holidays with a man who truly cared about her and his adorable little girl.

"I'd like nothing more than to spend the holidays with you and Katie. We can go to the church's Christmas program together. You were planning on going to it, weren't you?"

"You can count on it."

"Looking good."

Alyssa turned with a smile at the sound of Nathan's voice. "You think?" she said fretfully. "I'm starting to question my decision to add the waves."

"I like them," he said as he crossed the room to stand beside her. He studied the wall, his gaze fixed on the strip of dark blue she'd been hand painting waves across. "Much better than dancing bananas."

She elbowed him playfully in the ribs. "Be serious."

"I am," he said, shooting a teasing glance her way. Then he moved along the wall, admiring her work. "I was wondering if you had any plans for this evening."

"You didn't see enough of me last evening when we were working on the nativity?" she teased. "Actually, I was gonna go online and do some Christmas shopping," she said as she went back to painting. "It's how I do most of my shopping nowadays."

"Because you can't drive," he said, more a comment than a question.

She nodded.

"Why don't Katie and I take you shopping after work this evening? We could grab a bite to eat on the way."

Lowering her brush, she turned to him with a smile. "I'd like that. Speaking of Katie, I haven't seen her for a while. I think she got bored watching me paint squiggles on the wall."

"That's my daughter," he said with a chuckle. "Always has to be doing something. Last I saw her she was in the gym with Carter. He's hanging the netting from the hoops we put up yesterday and has appointed Katie his official basket tester."

"I'll bet she's loving that."

"Let me put it this way. My daughter's arms are gonna feel like limp noodles tonight." He glanced at his watch. "I'd best get back to work. Quitting time in one hour."

"So soon?" she gasped, her gaze shifting to the unfinished stripe that ran along the center of the wall. She still had half the length of that wall to finish adding waves to.

"Not soon enough," he said with a grin as he walked away whistling.

Smiling, she turned back to the section of waves she'd been working on.

"Am I mistaken or was that my brother who just came out of this room whistling a happy tune?" a deep voice asked.

She glanced back over her shoulder, watching as Carter's blurred form came into view. "It was."

He shook his head. "Thought maybe I was dreaming. Nice waves, by the way."

"Thanks," she replied with a smile. "Why would you think you were dreaming just because Nathan was whistling?"

"My brother never whistles," he replied. "At least, he hasn't since…" His words trailed off.

"Since Isabel died," she said in understanding.

"Yes." He leaned against a section of the wall she hadn't gotten to yet and crossed his arms. "Can I be honest with you, Alyssa?"

This sounded serious. She lowered the paintbrush she was holding. "I would hope you would be."

He smiled tenderly. "Because of you, Logan and I might actually get our brother back."

"I don't understand," she replied, confused by his words.

"Plain and simple, you've managed to knock down some of that emotional wall Nathan put up after Isabel's death, something no one else has been able to do for the past two years. And for that, Logan and I will be forever grateful. If there's ever anything we can do for you, all you have to do is ask." Pushing away from the wall, he started from the room.

"Carter," she called out.

His retreating footsteps ceased.

"He's taken down some of my walls, too."

He walked back over to her. "If things work out between the two of you the way I think they could, know that you'll be welcomed into our family with open arms." That said, he walked away, whistling the very same tune his brother had.

A family of her very own. It was something she had longed for all her life. Oh, how she wished she could hope for her and Nathan's relationship to grow in that direction. But how could she ever compete with the memory of his beloved wife? A woman Nathan had loved with all his heart. A woman who had been perfect in every way.

Unlike her.

Dressed and ready for her outing with Nathan and Katie that evening, Alyssa headed downstairs to wait. The twinkling lights of the Christmas tree drew her into the living room where it stood tucked away in the far corner. She moved toward it, drawn in by its warm, welcoming glow. It was the first evening since she'd been there that the tree had been lit.

The shining star at the top of the massive pine was only a few inches shy of the twelve-foot ceiling. Delicate glass ornaments dripped from nearly every branch, adding a wealth of color.

She thought about the tiny tinsel tree she'd bought with money she'd earned babysitting for a neighbor when she was thirteen. It had sat in her living room without lights and with only a few homemade paper ornaments because anything more would surely have weighed its frail, wiry branches down, possibly even broken them. How had she ever thought her tree beautiful?

Reaching out, she gingerly touched one of the tree's delicate ornaments. A deep burgundy heart trimmed in tiny gold flowers.

"Henry bought me that our first Christmas together."

Alyssa let her hand fall back to her side, embarrassed to have been caught so wistfully admiring the tree. "It's lovely." She glanced over as Doris came to stand next to her. "I hope you don't mind my…"

"Oh, don't fret, dear," the older woman said, her gaze moving up the beautifully decorated tree. "This room is intended to be a place for our guests to relax and enjoy. This lovely tree included."

"I didn't realize how beautiful it was," she admitted in awe.

"Perhaps because tonight is the first night we've had it lit since you've been here. We turn the tree lights on for the first time on this day every December in memory of our parents who were married on this date."

"That's such a touching way to honor your parents." Alyssa looked to the tree. "There are so many ornaments. And none of them are alike. Wherever did you find them all?"

"Each and every ornament on that tree is a tiny memory of the blessings our Lord has bestowed upon us over the years." She went on to point out ones that held particular meaning to her. "Nathan and his brothers gave me this one," she said, pointing toward the basket of kittens suspended by a bright red ribbon.

Alyssa felt a tug at her heart. "How wonderful it must be to have such meaningful ornaments to reminisce over."

"There's nothing quite like a tree filled with sentimental old ornaments to make a Christmas more special," Doris said with a wistful sigh. Then she glanced her way. "You don't have any special ones of your own you've collected?"

Alyssa shook her head.

The older woman smiled. "Well, it's never too late to start." Reaching up into the tree, she freed a crystal gift box and handed it to Alyssa.

She stared down at the ornament in her hand. "I can't accept this."

"Sure you can," Doris insisted. "'Tis the season for giving and this is my gift to you. In years to come, when you look back at it, know that it represents the selfless gift you gave to the folks of Braxton. Putting your own life on hold to come here and help give us back something we lost in that awful storm."

Tears filled Alyssa's eyes as she held the delicate, sparkling piece. "I'll treasure it forever. Thank you so very much."

"Oh, dear, I didn't mean to get you all misty-eyed right before your date with Nathan. Myrna is bound to cluck her tongue at me if I take you into the parlor all choked up."

She laughed softly, wiping a single tear from her face. "I'm fine. Really I am." How had a woman she'd known for a little over a week touch her more deeply than her own mother ever had? "And it's not a date. We're just friends."

"Whatever they're calling it these days, dear," the older woman said with a smile. "Now come on into the parlor for some tea before you go."

"But Nathan and Katie will be here any minute."

"If they get here before we're finished, we'll simply invite them in to join us for a cup."

It was hard to imagine Nathan Cooper, in all

his big, strong manliness, sitting down for a cup of tea served in antique china. Then again, the man did have a soft side that never failed to warm her heart.

With a nod, Alyssa followed her into the parlor where Myrna was setting out a plate of what she could only assume, thanks to her limited vision, were cookies.

"Perfect timing," Myrna said with a warm smile.

"Alyssa was admiring our tree."

"It's beautiful," Alyssa told her. "Your sister gave me this lovely ornament for my tree back home." She gingerly laid the crystal ornament on the table next to her teacup.

"We're helping her start her very own ornament collection," Doris explained. "Ours is her very first."

Myrna looked her way. "Really?" she asked, surprise in her tone.

"My mother was never one for decorating during the holidays. So there were no special keepsakes to pass down when she passed away." Truth was, any spare money her mother had left after paying bills went to buying more liquor and cigarettes. At least her mother had managed to keep a roof over their heads despite her addiction to alcohol, and for that she was grateful.

Looking across the table at the empathetic

expressions that had fallen over her hostesses' once beaming faces, she forced a bright smile. "I'll be sure to put this gift to good use. I love decorating my place in San Antonio for the holidays."

The doorbell rang and Alyssa's heart sped up. She started to rise, but Doris motioned for her to stay seated.

"You haven't finished your tea. I'll go bring your young man and his little girl inside."

"Tell Nathan we have cookies," Myrna called after her.

Her sister glanced back over her slightly stooped shoulder. "I think Alyssa's being here is all we need to entice the young man in."

Warmth filled her cheeks and it was still there when Doris led a grinning Nathan into the parlor.

"Ladies," he said with a polite nod. Then his gaze sought her out and his smile widened.

She returned his smile, then looked past him. "Where's Katie?"

"With Logan," he replied. "My brother called to tell her he was gonna go see some Disney movie and asked if she wanted to join him, then do a little Christmas shopping of their own."

"Logan was going to a Disney movie?" she repeated suspiciously. Nathan's brother going to watch an animated children's movie wasn't something she could quite picture in her mind.

"Oh, my," Doris said worriedly. "Your brother went to all that trouble to give the two of you some alone time and here we are keeping you from it."

Myrna looked at Nathan. "You two had best get going. We'll do tea another time."

"And just when I was eyeing that plate of cookies," Nathan said, feigning disappointment.

"We can take care of that," Doris said, scurrying off into the kitchen. A few seconds later, she returned carrying a small, plastic baggie, which she began filling up with cookies.

Smiling, Alyssa pushed away from the table and collected her precious gift. "I'll be right back down. Doris and Myrna gave me this lovely tree ornament to start my own special collection. I need to put it in my room and then we can go."

"That was kind of you," Nathan said to the sisters as they walked him out onto the porch to wait for Alyssa.

"We adore her," Myrna said.

Doris nodded. "She deserves a whole tree filled with special memories. Not just one from two eccentric old women."

"That she does," he agreed, turning as the screen door swung open behind him. "All set?"

Alyssa nodded happily. "Ready when you are."

"We'll leave the porch light on for you," Doris called out as he walked her out to the truck.

"Thank you," Alyssa hollered back, attempting to smother a giggle. Then she added in a hushed voice as he helped her up into the cab, "They are too cute."

"They are that," Nathan agreed, the cookie-filled sandwich bag Doris had given him dangling from his hand. Closing the passenger door, he rounded the truck, feeling like a teenager on his first date.

"Baby steps," he said to himself, knowing he needed to slow down, to rein in his growing feelings for Alyssa. But she'd breathed life into him and he didn't want to go back to just existing. For the first time in two years, she had him rethinking the way he'd been living his life. Especially when it came to his relationship with the Lord and the anger he'd been harboring toward Him. She even had him willingly doing something he would have avoided altogether if not for his daughter—going Christmas shopping.

Venturing out to a busy mall in the middle of December of all things. One he knew would be festively decorated for the Christmas holiday. A time that held some very painful memories for him. But like Katie, Alyssa deserved to experience those things. The holiday shopping trips. Picnics under the sun. The beauty of a waterfall. And so much more.

Smiling, he started the truck, shifted into gear and pulled away from the boardinghouse. "Would you like to grab something to eat first?"

"I think that might be a good idea. We need to talk and I doubt that's something we'll be able to do in private while walking through a crowded mall."

"We need to talk," he repeated with a sinking feeling. "Sounds serious." He glanced her way.

"To me, it is," she said, glancing his way. "If I'm being completely honest with you, I'm scared."

He certainly hadn't expected that. The last thing he wanted Alyssa to be was scared about anything. "I'm pulling over so we can talk this out."

"It can wait," she said, nibbling on her lower lip.

"We're on a back road with little or no traffic. It doesn't get any more private than this." Pulling off the road, he shut off the engine, undid his seat belt and then turned to face her. "Talk to me, Alyssa," he said, reaching for her hand. "What is it you're afraid of?"

She glanced down at his hand over hers. "Of anything beyond friendship." A frown immediately followed. "Not that you've implied you want more."

His searching eyes met hers. "And what if I do?"

"Nathan…"

"What if I do?" he repeated. "I've tried to focus on work. On Katie. On having a friendship with you and not wanting more. But my thoughts continually drift back to you. To us."

"Don't," she warned in a soft whisper, her gaze fixed on their joined hands.

"Is it the long-distance thing that worries you?" he said, his thumb caressing her hand. "Because I'm willing to find a way to make it work."

"It's so much more than that," she confessed with a sigh. "It's knowing that I'm not really what you're looking for. It's my fear of not being able to give Katie everything she needs. It's—"

"Shh…" he said, squeezing her hand. "I'm gonna stop you right there. First of all, I wasn't looking for anyone. Just ask my brothers. They know what my thoughts were on ever letting another woman into my life again. Then you came to town and everything changed. I find myself counting the hours until I see you at the rec center each morning, when I should be focused solely on the job I've been hired to do."

Her smile returned. "I could say the same thing."

He offered a tender smile. "Glad to hear it. And as far as my daughter's concerned, you are exactly what she needs in her life. You're smart. You're talented. You're strong in the face of adversity."

"Nathan," she said, blushing.

"I'm not done. You have one of the most giving hearts I have ever known. You're as beautiful inside as you are on the outside. I know we've talked about building our friendship, but I find myself wanting to give a relationship between us a chance."

She grew misty-eyed. "I want that, too. And since honesty is so important to me, there's one more admission I need to make."

"You're already married?" he teased.

"Not even close," she said, looking up at him. A tiny smile teased the corners of her mouth.

"Then there's nothing you can say that'll change my mind about wanting to date you."

"I can't remember the last time I dated. I'm not even sure I remember how to date." She lowered her gaze as if embarrassed by the fact.

She thought that was a bad thing? He was

relieved there was no one in her recent past to compete with for her affection. "I haven't dated anyone since Isabel," he admitted. "Looks like we'll be learning how to date again together."

*And since honesty is so important to me...*

Nathan sighed as he recalled her words. That honesty should go both ways. Had to go both ways for things between them to have any chance of working out long term. "While we're laying everything out on the table, I reckon it's only fair that you know what you're getting into with me. I'm not the man you think I am."

She looked up at him questioningly.

"I'm not the devout Christian I once was."

"I don't understand. You go to church every Sunday. You're helping to build the nativity scene for the church's Christmas program."

He frowned. "For Katie's sake."

She fell silent, contemplating his words. Then, she said softly, "You said *used to*. What changed things for you?"

He looked away, jaw tightening as he recalled the storm. The loss. The pain that followed. "Having Isabel and my parents taken from me, from Katie, in such a horrific way. How could my God, the one I'd put my trust in above all others, allow something like that to happen?"

She gave his hand a gentle squeeze. "I can't

even begin to imagine what you went through.
I only lost my vision."

"Only?" he said with a hollow chuckle. "It's
still a loss. My family. Your eyesight. It all cuts
deep."

"Maybe so, but I don't hold God responsible
for what happened to me. And as awful as what
happened to your family was, you need to know
that He loves them. You need to *believe*."

"I don't know if I can," he muttered, hating
that this one truth could change everything between them. "Can you accept me, knowing that
I might never find my way back?"

She smiled softly. "I accept you. Not in spite
of the possibility you might never find your
way back to Him, but because I have faith that
you will."

# Chapter Ten

"Daddy," Katie groaned, "I don't feel so well."

Nathan stopped what he was doing and crossed the room to where his daughter sat shivering in her coat on a makeshift bench. Placing a hand on her forehead, he frowned. She was warm to the touch.

"You feel feverish," he said, immediately worried that his baby girl was ill.

"But I don't want a fever," she whined. "I have work to do."

"Work can wait," he told her with a frown. "Were you feeling bad this morning when I woke you up?"

She nodded her reply.

"Honey, why didn't you say something?" He would have kept her at home. Not dragged her into the rec center.

"I already told you why, Daddy. I gotta be here to help Alyssa."

"Not if you're sick," he told her, yet couldn't help but feel proud at her determination to see a job she'd been given through to the end. "You should be home, tucked snugly in your bed."

Katie had spent the past several days tagging along after Alyssa and loving every minute of it. While he'd worried at first about his daughter getting too attached, especially knowing she was looking for something he wasn't prepared to give her, everything had changed. He loved watching the two of them "working" and playing together. His daughter was happier than he'd seen her in a very long time.

Carter stepped up beside him. "She okay?"

"I think she has a fever."

"Let me see, kiddo." He bent to place a hand to her brow. "Yep, she feels pretty warm."

The front door opened and Alyssa stepped inside with her usual cheery smile. He'd offered to give her a ride to work when they'd talked on the phone earlier that morning, but she'd insisted on walking to work because it was such a nice day. "Good morning!"

"Morning, yes," Nathan muttered. "The good part is questionable."

"Why? What's the matter?"

"Katie's not feeling so well," Carter answered for him.

Setting her work tote on the floor by the door, she hurried over to them. "Ah, sweetie, what's wrong?"

"My tummy hurts."

"She's feverish," Nathan said as he studied his daughter's flushed cheeks and glazed eyes.

Alyssa knelt in front of her, pressing the back of her hand to Katie's cheek. "You poor baby. You must have picked up a bug somewhere." She looked up at him. "Why on earth did you bring her in today if she wasn't feeling well?"

"I didn't know," he replied, feeling as though he had failed Katie as a father. How had he not noticed the telltale flush in her cheeks?

"Where does your tummy hurt?" Alyssa asked her.

"Right here," his daughter replied, pointing at her stomach. "And I'm itchy."

"Itchy?" all three adults repeated in unison.

Katie nodded, her tiny bottom lip pouting.

Alyssa looked up at Nathan. "Is she on any medication? Something she might be having a reaction to?"

"No."

"Can I take a look at your tummy, sweetie?" Alyssa asked calmly.

Katie lifted the bottom of her shirt to display

several red spots. Alyssa leaned in to inspect the raised red flesh more closely.

A rush of panic moved through Nathan as he eyed the angry red welts. "I need to get her to the hospital."

"The hospital?" Katie exclaimed, her bottom lip trembling. "Why, Daddy? I don't wanna go there again."

"I know, honey, but you've got spider bites we need to have looked at."

Alyssa sat back and reached out, placing a calming hand on his arm. "I don't think they're spider bites."

"Then what are they?" Nathan insisted with a worried frown.

"Look closer," Alyssa said softly. "Tell me if you think they look more like little blisters than bites. Any puncture holes?"

"No puncture holes," he said, his voice tight with worry.

"Watery blisters?" she repeated.

He frowned, worry creasing his brow. "Yes."

She offered him a reassuring smile. "I'd say Katie has all the symptoms of chicken pox."

"Chicken pox?" he exclaimed, eyes widening as he stared down at his daughter's polka-dotted tummy.

She nodded. "We had several cases of it at the rec center last year in San Antonio. Turn around, sweetie," she said to Katie, lifting her shirt to reveal more of the telltale red specks on his daughter's lower torso. "More watery blisters?"

"Yes." He lifted his gaze to meet hers. "But how did she get the chicken pox?" Nathan asked. "She hasn't been around anyone that has them."

"Jennalynn had polka dots on her when she came over to draw chalk pictures on Granny Timmons' sidewalk with me," Katie said sleepily.

Surely she would have been sick before now if that's really what this was. "Honey, that was over two weeks ago," Nathan pointed out.

"And probably when she contracted them," Alyssa said knowingly. "If I remember right, the incubation period is between ten to twenty-one days."

"I should have known something was wrong," Nathan said with a frown.

"You're not a doctor," Carter said. "Now that we know she's sick, we need to get her home and in bed."

"I'll take her home," Nathan said.

"I'd have Audra come get her, but I don't know if Mason and Lily have had the chicken pox yet. Or her for that matter," he added with a frown.

"She's pregnant," Alyssa said. "Better off not

taking the chance either way." She stood and turned to Nathan. "Chicken pox is fairly contagious. I suggest making sure your crew has all had it."

"I will. Carter and I have already had it. And you?" he asked worriedly.

"I've had it, too."

Relief swept through him. Katie being sick already had him turned inside out. If Alyssa were to get sick, too, he didn't know what he'd do.

"I'll let the guys know," Carter announced.

"I'm taking Katie home," Nathan said, scooping his daughter up in his arms.

"Take care of Katie. I'll hold the fort down here until you're able to come back to work."

"I'd be happy to stay with Katie at your place while you work," Alyssa offered, her gaze fixed on Katie's shivering form.

"Can she, Daddy?" his fevered daughter asked hopefully.

"I can't ask you to do that," Nathan said, shaking his head in refusal.

"I don't mind at all," she told him. "I've already had the virus, so that won't be an issue." She offered a sympathetic smile to Katie who looked ready to fall asleep at any moment. "And I can work on my computer while she sleeps, which will probably be most of the day once we get some medicine in her for that fever. If you don't already have some at your place, we should pick up some oatmeal bath on our way there. It'll help to soothe her discomfort. And you should call Katie's doctor to see what anti-histamine he recommends we give her for the itching."

She looked up to find Nathan and Carter staring at her. "I'm sorry," she quickly apologized. "I wasn't trying to overstep. You—"

"Should take her up on her offer," Carter said, cutting her off. "Sounds to me like Katie would be in excellent hands with Alyssa."

Nathan looked at her as if in awe. "I couldn't agree more."

"I'll go talk to the men," Carter said. "You'd best get my little Katydid home."

"Going right now." He started for the door, his daughter held so lovingly in his arms.

Alyssa grabbed her work tote and hurried after his departing form. "What about your coat?" she called after him. Thankfully, Katie had been wearing hers.

"Don't need it," he replied, his steps not faltering.

Was the man crazy? It was freezing outside. However, she managed to keep her protests to herself. Nathan was under enough stress as it was. His focus at that moment was on getting his sick daughter home and into her bed. So she grabbed his jacket on the way out, determined to have him put it on as soon as he had Katie settled in the truck's cab.

After stopping at the local drugstore where Alyssa ran in to pick up the items they needed for Katie's care, they headed out of town. Katie had fallen fast asleep beside Alyssa in her booster seat.

Alyssa glanced down at the head resting against her. Sun shining in through the passenger window glinted off the sleeping child's dark curls. "I would give anything for hair like hers," she said softly, gently stroking the silken strands.

"She has her mother's hair," Nathan said, his gaze shifting to his sleeping daughter. "Her eyes, too."

"Your wife must have been beautiful."

He hesitated in answering, his attention shifting back to the road ahead.

"It's okay," she told him. "Isabel was a very important part of your lives. Always will be, if only in memory. I want you to be able to talk about her. For your sake and for Katie's."

"Yes," he said. "She was beautiful." Then he glanced her way with a sincere smile. "She would have liked you."

"Thank you for saying that," she said, touched

more deeply than he could ever know. "That means a lot to me."

They fell into a comfortable silence for the remainder of the drive home.

When they arrived, Nathan came around to the passenger side of the truck. Together they lifted Katie out until she was once again in her daddy's arms.

Alyssa followed them inside.

"There's bottled water in the fridge," he told her. "Would you mind grabbing one for Katie so we can get her medicine into her?"

He said *we*, not I. She smiled softly. "Not at all. Get Katie to bed and I'll be right in."

She grabbed a bottle of water from the fridge, and then went in search of Katie's bedroom.

She found it at the end of the upstairs hallway. The room, definitely a little girl's room, was filled with brightly colored stuffed animals. A large dollhouse stood in the far corner. Beside it sat a basket filled with dolls to play with inside the miniature house. A cotton-candy-pink ruffled valance hung over a small bay window that overlooked the tree-lined backyard.

"I've got the water," she said.

"Honey," he said against Katie's ear, "you need to wake up. Daddy's got to get you ready for bed."

She stirred with a sleepy grumble.

"Here," Alyssa said, setting the bottle of water down on the nightstand. "Let me help you." She slid Katie's boots from her feet and set them on the floor near the foot of the bed. Then she moved to help Nathan with Katie's coat.

Once they had changed her into her night-gown, had gotten the medicine into her and had settled her into bed, Nathan drew the sheet up over Katie. Then he grabbed for the Disney Princesses comforter folded neatly across the foot of the twin bed, but Alyssa stilled his hand.

"She's got a fever," she whispered. "You don't want her getting overheated. Do you have a lighter blanket?"

He nodded. "In the hall closet."

"I'll get it."

When she returned, Alyssa paused in the doorway, her heart melting as Nathan bent to place a tender kiss on his daughter's fevered brow. "You're gonna be fine, Cupcake." His hands smoothed the sheet covering her, his muscular shoulders flexing beneath the flannel work shirt he wore. His physical strength a stark contradiction to his gentleness.

Smiling, she stepped into the room, unfolding the blanket as she went. "How is she?" she whispered.

"Sleeping." He backed away and stood for a long moment watching over his daughter.

Alyssa placed a comforting hand on his arm. "She's gonna be okay, just a little uncomfortable for the next week or so."

"I know," he said with a nod. "It's just so hard seeing her sick."

"I can imagine, considering all she's been through."

He turned to look at her. "You've been really good for her."

"I care about her," she said softly. *I care about you.*

"Did you eat before coming in to work?"

She hesitated before shaking her head, not wanting him to have something else to concern himself over. "No."

"Come on," he said, taking her hand. "Let's go fix a couple of sandwiches and have an early lunch before I head back to the rec center."

"Do you have time?"

He smiled. "Carter can handle things until I get back."

They went downstairs to the kitchen, where Nathan released her hand and went to open the fridge. "Turkey or ham?"

"Turkey's fine. Can I do something to help?"

"Paper plates are in the cupboard to the left of the window," he said as he reached into the fridge for a package of lunch meat. "Tomato?"

"Sounds good." She lifted two plates off the stack and set them onto the counter.

Nathan stepped past her, pulling a loaf of bread from a nearby drawer. "I'll give Mildred a call this afternoon and see if she has any idea when she might be coming home."

"You don't have to do that," she assured him as he moved to the counter to start making their sandwiches. "I have the layout for all the rooms, so I can do most of my work on my laptop from here. I'd hate for Mildred to feel like she needs to rush back to Braxton when she's already promised her sister that she'll be there to help her out until she's back on her feet."

"I suppose you're right."

"I just know how much it means to have someone there with you when you're recovering. To offer you support both physically and emotionally."

He glanced her way. "I wish I could have been there for you."

That touched her. "I had Erica."

"I'm glad." With a smile, he went back to making their sandwiches. "And you're right. If she knew about Katie being sick, Mildred would drop everything to race home and be with her. And that wouldn't be fair to her sister. I just wish…" His words trailed off.

"Are you concerned that I won't be able to

take care of Katie?" she heard herself asking in a tone that bordered on hurt. But she couldn't help it. It wouldn't be the first time someone thought she was less capable of doing something because of her visual impairment.

His gaze shot up to meet hers. "Not for a second," he said in all sincerity. "I saw how you responded at the rec center when you knew she was sick. I panicked. You remained calm. You had a fairly good idea of what was going on with my daughter, while I was imagining all sorts of things that could be wrong with her. I just wish I was better at handling this sort of thing. But I promise there is no doubt in my mind, whatsoever, that my daughter will be well cared for and safe in your hands."

Tears pooled in her eyes. "That means so much to me."

He drew her to him. "And *you* mean the world to me. I'm so glad you came into our lives." His gaze fell to her lips and her pulse began to race. She was certain he'd been about to kiss her when his cell phone rang. Releasing her, he pulled his cell from the front pocket of his jeans and then looked up at her, saying, "It's Logan."

She nodded.

"She's sleeping," Nathan told his brother. Then he glanced Alyssa's way. "Thanks for the offer, but Katie's in capable hands. Besides, we might need you to help out with some of the finishing touches to the rec center." He nodded. "Okay, see you in a few." He disconnected. "Carter called Logan to tell him about Katie, so he was calling to offer himself up as Katie's temporary caretaker."

"Carter didn't tell him I was gonna to be staying with her?"

"He did," he said as he walked over to the pantry to grab a half-empty bag of potato chips. "But Logan thought you might be needed at the rec center."

"That was thoughtful of him, considering he has his own business to run, as well."

Nathan shook a small pile of chips out onto each plate. "Contrary to the flirt you've come to know, my brother does have a responsible side." He motioned toward the fridge. "If you wanna grab a couple of bottles of water for us, I'll carry our plates out to the table."

"Sounds good." She walked over to get their drinks. When she stepped out into the dining room area, Nathan was nowhere to be found. Her gaze shifted to the plates on the table and then toward the open living room. Had Katie cried out?

She set the bottles down and had just started for the stairs when Nathan came down the steps. "Is she okay?"

"She's fine," he said as he walked her back to the table and their awaiting lunch. "Still fast asleep."

Alyssa understood his need to check on his daughter. Katie was all he had left of Isabel. "God will watch over her."

He looked as if he wanted to say something in response. Instead, he pulled a chair out from under the table and motioned for her to have seat. "Let's eat."

She smiled up at him as he walked to the chair kitty-corner from hers. At least, he hadn't dismissed the likelihood of God watching over Katie. Even if she'd seen the doubt on his face for a fleeting moment. It was a start, no matter how small, of his finding his way back to the Lord. The thought warmed her.

They sat in silence for several minutes as they ate. Or maybe as she ate. The turkey sandwich and potato chips on Nathan's plate remained mostly untouched.

Alyssa reached out, covering his hand with her own much smaller one. "Are you okay?"

His worried frown deepened. "I shouldn't be going back to work. My place is here with Katie."

"If you feel that strongly about it, then call Carter and tell him you won't be coming back today," she said, fully understanding his need to be with his daughter.

"It'll put us behind schedule."

"Then it puts us behind," she said. "You have to follow your heart."

"Katie is so excited for the Christmas Eve party," he said with a frown. "If we get behind, there's a chance that might not happen. And then there's the dedication…" He glanced in the direction of the hallway. "You really think she'll sleep for a while?"

"Most of the day, I would guess," she assured him.

His jaw clenched as he struggled with what to do. Finally, he looked her way. "You have my cell number?"

She smiled. "I do."

"And you'll call me if you need anything?"

"I will."

"Then I'll go back to the rec center and see that we get the job done—for Katie." He pushed away from the table and stood.

"You haven't finished your lunch."

"I'm not very hungry," he replied. "I'll eat it when I get home this evening."

"I'll walk you out." Together they started for the front door, his hand laced through hers. The slight tension she felt in his grasp was that of a man torn between what he needed to do and what he wanted to do.

"There's apple juice and iced tea in the fridge," he said when they reached the door. "And chicken noodle soup and snacks in the pantry. Help yourself to whatever you need for you or Katie." His worried frown had deepened, no doubt brought about by the thought of leaving his sick little girl. He pulled open the door and stood there. "I'll try to come home early."

She reached up to touch his cheek, smiling softly. "Katie and I will be fine. Do what you need to do. We'll see you this evening."

"You'll call if her fever gets any worse?"

"Of course."

Hand on the doorknob, he paused. "Alyssa…"

"Yes?"

He bent to kiss her cheek. "Thank you." And then he was gone.

Hand pressed to her cheek, Alyssa walked over to the window, watching as the blur she knew to be Nathan climbed into his truck and drove away. A slow smile spread across her face as she turned away and remained there as she moved toward the stairs to check on Katie.

She was still fast asleep. Alyssa stood at her bedside, watching her for a long while, relieved to see that the little girl's shivering had eased.

Like Nathan, she hated seeing Katie ill. She'd come to adore her. No, she'd come to love her.

*I could be her new mother.*

The thought settled in, filling her with both elation and trepidation. She would never try to replace Isabel. But if things worked out between her and Nathan down the road, she would become a very important part of Katie's life. She would be responsible for helping to guide her in both life and in faith as she grew into a young woman, for nurturing her, for doing all the wonderful things Erica did with her children. Mother things.

But she wasn't Erica. There were so many things she couldn't do that other mothers could. Like drive Katie to birthday parties for her friends. Like riding bikes any farther than the driveway because she might not see a car coming until it was too late. Even playing hide and seek would be a real challenge. What if what she had to offer Katie wasn't enough? She didn't think she could bear failing Katie. Or Nathan.

The elation that had filled her only moments before faded, leaving behind a growing sense of panic. She needed to talk to Erica. Her best friend was a straight shooter who told it like it was. She also understood the insecurities Alyssa had worked so hard to get past since her accident.

Stepping from the room, she drew the door shut, leaving it slightly ajar in case Katie awoke and needed something. Then she went out to the kitchen where she'd left her tote and purse. Pulling out her cell, she dialed her friend's number and then began searching through the kitchen drawers for some plastic wrap to cover Nathan's nearly untouched meal with.

Erica answered on the second ring. "Hey you!"

"Hey."

"Uh-oh. Do I detect a hint of unhappiness in your voice?"

"Only because I'm worried about Katie. She's come down with chicken pox."

"The poor baby."

"I offered to take care of her while Nathan goes back to work on the rec center."

"What about your work?"

"The flooring that Nathan, Carter and I decided on has already been ordered and should be in the day after tomorrow. His crew has been busy painting the rooms with the colors I chose. Tables are picked out for the cafeteria and the art room. All I need to do is order the light fixtures for the lobby, rec center office and for above the mirror-backed counters in the locker rooms. I can do that from here."

"Sounds like you have everything under control on your end."

"I do," she said proudly. If only she were as in control of her emotions.

"Excuse me one moment," her friend said. "Huck Benson, if that hamster gets loose again, he's gonna have to find himself a new place to live!"

Alyssa couldn't help but smile. "Hamster troubles?"

"Sorry," her friend apologized. "Things have been in a bit of an uproar here."

"Why? What happened?"

"When I got home from the grocery store this morning everyone, my husband included, was in a panic because Huck's hamster had gone missing. We went on a mad search to find it before our cat did."

"Apparently, you found it," she said, her own concerns temporarily pushed aside. She knew how much Huck loved his furry, little pet.

"Thankfully, yes. He was in Cecilia's bed-room, dining on Cheerios."

"What?"

"My daughter decided Mr. Cuddles was too cramped in his hamster cage and moved him into her doll house where she fed him the rest of the cereal she'd been snacking on."

"Oh, the joys of motherhood," she said with a snort of laughter.

"Laugh all you want now, my friend, but one

of these days I'm gonna be the one laughing at the mischief your children get into."

*Her children.* The reminder of why she'd called her friend to begin with had her frowning once more.

"Hello? Alyssa?"

"I'm here," she said with a sigh. "And funny you should mention children. I was having a moment of panic over the possibility of being someone's mother someday."

"Are you referring to Katie?"

"Her or any other children I might have." And she would willingly take however many God chose to bless her with. "But I can't help but wonder if I won't be able to give them everything they deserve."

"Like a mother who loves them with her whole heart?" her friend asked. "One who would protect them, guide them and teach them. One who would show them what it means to stay strong and hold on to their faith, even in the face of adversity."

"Erica…"

"Don't 'Erica' me," she said. "You are all of those things. And any child will be more than blessed to have you in their life."

Oh, how she prayed her friend was right. Because she never wanted to fail someone she loved as her mother had failed her.

# Chapter Eleven

Seeing a movement out the corner of her eye, Alyssa looked up from the sketch she was working on. "Katie!" She pushed away from the kitchen table and walked over to the sleepy-eyed child. "What are you doing out of bed?"

"I'm thirsty."

Her face looked a little flushed. Then again, the tiny, red blisters that had popped up over her cheeks and forehead added to the extra color she saw in Katie's face. Alyssa placed a hand to her brow, fearing the fever she'd been without the past two days had returned. Blessedly, it hadn't.

"Why don't I walk you back to bed and then I'll fix you a glass of lemonade?"

She shook her head, adding in a tiny whine, "I don't wanna be in my bed. Not by myself."

"Why not?"

"'Cause I had a bad dream."

"What about, sweetie?" she asked in a calming tone.

"The storm."

"But the rain shower has passed." It had rained most of the day, but not hard enough to bring about nightmares.

"Not that storm," Katie said, adding in a hushed voice, "The tornado."

Alyssa didn't miss the shudder that passed through Katie's tiny form at her mention of the storm that had ripped Braxton apart two years ago. "Oh, honey," she said, dropping to her knees in front of her. She drew her into her arms and held her tight. "I wouldn't let anything happen to you. It was just a dream. It's over now."

"It'll come back," she said.

"The dream?"

"And the tornado," she replied, her bottom lip trembling. "I don't wanna be crushed again."

Alyssa ran her hand in soothing circles over her tiny back. Her first instinct had been to promise her that such a storm would never happen again, but no one had any say over where and when natural disasters would take place. Only God knew what the future held. So she settled for, "That was a rare storm. One that's not likely to happen here ever again."

Katie didn't look convinced. "Will you sit with me till I go back to sleep?"

Alyssa glanced toward the open laptop and the paper-strewn table and then back to Katie with a sympathetic smile. "Of course I will, sweetie. Have a seat on the sofa while I go get you that drink."

"Okay."

"Would you like me to fix you a snack before you lie back down?"

"No, thank you," Katie replied with a tired yawn. "I'm just thirsty."

"I'll be right back." Alyssa hurried into the kitchen, her heart heavy for the little girl whose dreams should have been filled with rainbows and butterflies, but were instead filled with memories of that terrible day.

She stepped up to the stove, leaning close to read the clock. It was just after five, which meant she'd been working on ideas and sketches for nearly three hours straight. Nathan had called sometime around four o'clock to check on Katie and to see if Alyssa minded him sticking around the site a little longer. Apparently the inspector was running behind on his appointments due to bad road conditions. Of course, it hadn't been a problem for her. She was actually getting a lot done while taking care of Katie. And when his daughter wasn't sleeping, they spent a lot of time playing board games, watching princess videos and just talking.

Yet, in all that time, Katie had never mentioned having nightmares. It sounded as if this hadn't been the first she'd had them. Did Nathan know? They were definitely something he needed to be aware of.

Alyssa filled a glass with ice and then the lemonade she and Katie had made yesterday. Then she returned to the living room where Katie sat waiting for her. "Here you go, honey."

Katie took several long swallows, then started for her room. "Where's my daddy?"

"He's still at work. But he called to check on you."

"Will he be home soon?"

"He needs to stay a little later at the rec center, but he said to tell you he was gonna stop by Big Dog's tonight to pick us up dinner and your favorite treat."

"A milk shake!" she squealed, her sleepy eyes lighting up.

Alyssa nodded with a smile, taking the glass from Katie's hand. "Now let's get you back in that bed so you'll be rested up for when your daddy comes home."

Alyssa and Katie went upstairs to her bedroom, where she climbed up onto the soft mattress and settled back onto her pillow. "You won't leave, will you?"

"I'll be right here." Setting the glass on the nightstand, she pulled Katie's covers up. Then she walked around the bed and settled onto the mattress beside her, resting her back against the headboard.

Katie snuggled up against her, once again fighting sleep.

Alyssa pushed the dark curls from her cheek. "Just close your eyes and sleep. I promise to keep the bad dreams away."

Katie looked up, her dark eyes hopeful. "Like Daddy does?"

That meant Nathan was aware of the nightmares Katie had. She smiled down at her. "How does your daddy keep them away?"

"He sings."

Alyssa's eyes widened. "He sings?"

"Uh-huh. Daddy says it'll scare all the bad dreams away."

Alyssa couldn't contain her grin. Nathan Cooper was a man of many talents. "Well, I don't think I can compete with your daddy's singing, but I can make a really mean face guaranteed to scare away any bad dreams."

"Can I see it?"

"Here goes." She scrunched up her face and

pursed her lips, the effort eliciting giggles from Katie. "What's so funny?"

"You don't look scary. You look like my daddy did when Uncle Carter dared him to eat a lemon."

Alyssa smothered a giggle. Ah, the information one could glean from a child. "Well, lucky for you bad dreams fear sour lemon faces *and* bad singing. Now close your eyes and go to sleep."

Within minutes, Katie was sound asleep, her little fingers curled into the comforter Alyssa had drawn up around her.

Caring for Katie this past week had been one of the most fulfilling experiences of her life. And she felt closer to Nathan than she'd ever dreamed possible. Life was good. Closing her eyes, she said a quick prayer of thanks to God for sending her on this path. Then her thoughts went back to Nathan, envisioning that big, strong man sitting patiently by Katie's side, singing her nightmares away as his daughter drifted off to sleep.

The rec center inspection had taken a lot longer than Nathan had expected, but at least it was done. They'd passed without a single violation. Now he could go home to his girl. *His girls.* He liked the sound of that. Liked having Alyssa there to greet him when he came home every day. Liked feeling like he had a family again.

He glanced at the clock on the dash. It was only 7:10 p.m., but it felt a lot later thanks to the early winter sunset. Beside him on the passenger seat, sat the carryout bag from Big Dog's. Alyssa had been incredible, not only taking care of his daughter, but fixing dinner for the three of them every night. Tonight, however, he was bringing dinner home to his girls. Hot dogs, fries and thick milk shakes.

Nathan turned onto the drive that led to his place. The kitchen and living room lights were on, but the rest of the house was dark. He pulled into the back garage and cut the engine. Then, grabbing the bag filled with their dinner, he went inside.

Closing the back door, he set the carryout bag on the kitchen counter, then shrugged out of his coat, hanging it from a hook by the door. So much for his family greeting him. Katie must still be asleep. Alyssa had said she'd been asleep when he'd called earlier.

After placing the shakes in the freezer, he started walking through the house in search of his girls. Alyssa's laptop and notes were spread out across the kitchen table, but she was nowhere to be seen. He made his way up to his daughter's room where the Cinderella lamp cast a soft glow across the double bed.

There they were. Katie fast asleep, her slender arm curled snugly around Alyssa's waist as she burrowed up against her. Alyssa's head tipped downward, her face covered by a curtain of coppery hair.

"Sorry I'm so late getting home," he said in a whisper.

No response.

He stepped closer. "Alyssa?"

Her soft, even breathing told him she was asleep, as well. He hated to wake them, but the hot dogs and fries wouldn't be too tasty cold. He walked around to Alyssa's side of the bed and reached out, gently pushing her hair away from her face. Then he whispered, "Dinner's here, darlin'."

She stirred, her head lifting as she slowly awakened. Her lashes fluttered open and then a startled gasp escaped her lips.

"Shh…" he said. "It's just me."

"Nathan?"

"Yes."

Coming more fully awake, she smiled up at him. "I didn't hear you come in."

"I figured as much." His gaze shifted to his sleeping daughter. "How is she?"

"No fever and the oatmeal baths seem to be helping with the itching."

He nodded, relieved to hear his daughter hadn't been suffering too much.

She looked down at his daughter with a slight frown. "Some dream chaser I am."

"Excuse me?"

Meeting his gaze once more, she said, her voice low, "Katie had a bad dream earlier. I was supposed to be watching over her and keeping the nightmares away. And what do I do? I fall asleep."

Not again. Would the nightmares ever fully go away? The therapist had told him they would eventually come with less frequency and at some point might go away altogether. But it would take time. Hard to swallow for a man wanting his daughter to feel safe always.

"Thank you for sitting with her. I'm sure you had things you needed to be doing."

"Not really," she admitted. "I managed to get a lot more done today than I had hoped to, so I had plenty of time to spare."

He frowned. "I hate to wake her. She's sleeping so soundly."

"I don't think you'd hear the end of it if you didn't," she told him. "Katie's expecting that milk shake I told her you were bringing home for her."

"I suppose we ought to get her up then. Logan will be by in a little over an hour to take you home." His brothers had been taking turns picking Alyssa up at the boardinghouse in the mornings and bringing her out to his place, where she'd stay with Katie while he went to work. Then either Carter or Logan would take Alyssa back to the boardinghouse after dinner each evening, allowing Nathan to spend more time with her than what little they were able to share during his all-too-brief afternoon lunch breaks.

Alyssa gave Katie a gentle nudge. "Katie, your daddy's home."

"Time to wake up, Cupcake," he joined in. "Dinner's waiting."

His daughter stirred, then stretched with a big yawn before opening her eyes. The minute she saw him in the lamplight, she untangled herself from Alyssa and threw back the covers. "Daddy!"

A smile pulled at his mouth. "Hey there, sleepyhead."

Katie scrambled to her feet, launching herself over Alyssa's legs and into his arms.

He caught her easily, shifting her around to rest on his hip. "How's my little chicken today?"

Hands clasped around his neck, she tipped

her head back with a groan. "I told you before. I'm not a chicken. I got the chicken pox. That's different."

Alyssa slipped from the bed to join them. "I don't know, Katie. With all those polka dots you have, I'm thinking you might be part leopard."

Laughing, they made their way downstairs to the dining room where Nathan set Katie down onto one of the chairs.

"Let me clean up my mess," Alyssa said, hurrying to scoop up the notes and sketches that were strewn about the table.

"I'll go grab the food." Nathan stepped into the kitchen, grabbed the shakes from the freezer and the carryout bag from the counter, then headed back out to the dining room.

"Which one's my shake?" Katie asked excitedly.

His gaze dropped down to the Styrofoam disposable cups. "Let's see…this one says Strawberry," he said, reading the lid where the flavor of each of the shakes had been handwritten across it.

She looked up at him. "But I wanted chocolate."

His brow lifted. "Chocolate? But I thought—"

"That's exactly what he brought you," Alyssa said. "I thought I'd give strawberry a try and see how I like it."

He looked at her questioningly. When he'd called to tell her he was bringing dinner home and to ask what flavor of shake she preferred, she'd requested chocolate.

"You'll like it," Katie assured her. "It's my second favorite."

What had his daughter said about it being a woman's prerogative to change her mind? It appeared such a thing was a common occurrence—for all women. Alyssa's kind gesture endeared her to him all the more. He would have given up his own shake to make his daughter happy, but he'd ordered a peanut butter shake for himself.

"Are you sure?" he asked Alyssa.

"I like to think of myself as the adventurous type," she told him with a smile as she reached for the cup marked Strawberry.

He handed Katie the chocolate one and then passed out the disposable containers that held their dinners in them. Then he looked to Alyssa. "Would you like to say a prayer before we eat?"

"I will! I will!" his daughter volunteered excitedly.

"That would be lovely," Alyssa told her with a smile.

Katie folded her hands together and closed her eyes. "Dear God, thank you for the yummy milk shake I'm about to drink. And for bringing Alyssa here. Amen."

Nathan met Alyssa's gaze, a grin tugging at his mouth. "Amen."

Alyssa smiled. "Amen."

Katie popped open her dinner container and dug into her fries.

Nathan had just taken a bite of his hot dog when Katie announced, "Alyssa snores."

Both he and Alyssa stopped midbite to look at her.

"What?" he managed around the mouthful of hot dog he had yet to swallow.

"Not loud like you do," his daughter explained. "Just tiny, little snores."

Alyssa's face colored. "I guess I have Rhett to blame for that."

"Rhett?" he repeated with a curious tilt of his head.

"He's Miss Myrna and Miss Doris's kitty," Katie told him with a smile.

Alyssa nodded. "He likes to play at night and one of his favorite games is tapping your face with his paw while you're sleeping."

Katie giggled. "That's silly."

Silly wasn't what he'd call being awakened from sleep in the middle of the night by a frisky cat. "Why don't you shut him out of the room?"

"I tried, but he sits outside the door and meows.

It's easier to let him in and pull a pillow over my head until he gets bored and leaves."

"No wonder you drifted off earlier," he said with a frown. "You need to be getting your rest, too."

"Please don't worry about me. I'm fine."

"I always concern myself when it comes to people I care about."

Katie nodded in agreement. "And Daddy really likes you. Don't you, Daddy?"

He smiled, meeting Alyssa's gaze. "Yes, Cupcake. I really like her. I like her a whole lot." More than he ever imagined he could care for another woman after Isabel. And for the first time since he'd begun having feelings for Alyssa, he felt no guilt. His brothers were right. Isabel would have wanted him to move on. To be happy. Alyssa had given him that and so much more.

Katie stepped from the bathroom in her plush pink princess robe. Now that she was feeling better, she had begun to bathe herself again. Alyssa would fix her special oatmeal bath and then wait for her in the hall.

She walked Katie to her room. "Let's see how that tummy is looking."

Katie raised her nightshirt, revealing her lightly speckled stomach. "They don't itch anymore."

That was a good thing. But her trunk and limbs still needed to be monitored for any new blisters. Kneeling on the floor in front of her, she leaned in to inspect her as best she could. Most of the blisters had finally scabbed over. She glanced up at Katie with a smile. "No new blisters that I can see, but we'll have your daddy double-check when he gets home tonight."

"So I'm all better?" Katie said excitedly.

"Another day or two and you should be able to leave the house. We'd hate to risk letting you around other children too soon and maybe getting them sick."

"Another day or two?" she whined. "That's too long."

She of all people understood Katie's restlessness. Those long, seemingly endless days she'd spent in the hospital and then in rehab after her car accident had verged on unbearable. "I know how hard this is for you, sweetie. But you wouldn't wanna risk giving the chicken pox to some other little boy or girl, would you?"

Katie shook her head. "Can we go outside?"

"Sweetie, it's too chilly out today. And they're calling for rain this evening. That means the air outside is probably damp. Not good for someone who recently recovered from a fever."

Katie sighed. Her pale, dotted face held a look of both misery and longing as her gaze drifted to the large picture window and the yard outside. "I wish I had my own dog to play with like Uncle Carter got for Mason and Lily."

Poor thing. Though her fever was long gone and chances were she was no longer contagious, to be on the safe side she was still confined to the house. Another day or so and Nathan should feel comfortable bringing Katie in to work with him again. Thankfully, none of Nathan's work crew had come down with the virus and things were moving along pretty close to schedule.

"Tell you what," Alyssa said, hoping her idea would cheer Katie up. "Since your daddy is too busy to decorate for the holidays, why don't you and I surprise him and do it for him?"

Katie gasped, her eyes widening in excitement. "Really?"

Alyssa smiled, relishing in the look of pure joy that had come over Katie's little face. She nodded. "It can be our special Christmas gift to your daddy."

"Yay!"

"Do you know where your daddy keeps the Christmas decorations?"

Her little head bobbed up and down. "In the roof."

"The roof?" Then it dawned on her. "Do you mean in the attic?"

She nodded enthusiastically.

"Well, if we're gonna surprise your daddy before he gets home we had better get started." The thought of giving Nathan a warm, cheerful, festive home to come back to after a long day's work had her smiling. Part of Christmas was giving to others and this was one way for her to give back to Nathan and Katie for accepting her into their lives and making her feel needed for the first time in years. Even loved, despite Nathan's never having said as much. As far as she was concerned, words were just words. Nathan had made her feel loved in so many other ways.

Taking Katie's hand, they ventured upstairs and down the hallway to where a rectangle-shaped panel above indicated the entrance to the attic. Letting go of Katie's hand, she reached up to grab the knotted pull rope hanging from one end of the door panel.

"Step back, sweetie," she warned as she pulled on the rope, lowering the narrow door. Then she grabbed for the folded steps and carefully opened them. Then she turned to Katie. "Wait down here while I go see what I can find."

"But I wanna help," she said with that adorable little pout her father couldn't resist. Unfortunately for Katie, Alyssa could. At least, when it meant keeping her safe.

"You will," she quickly assured her. "But with the decorating, not carrying heavy boxes down these wobbly stairs. You need to save your strength." She glanced toward the opening in the ceiling above her. Hopefully, she'd be able to find what they were looking for.

Three hours later, Katie was fast asleep in her bed, exhausted from their afternoon spent decorating. It had all been worth it. The house looked beautiful. Lights had been strung across the fireplace mantel with Katie's bright pink princess stocking hung on one side and Nathan's on the other. Katie had proudly informed her that she had made her daddy's stocking for him. The crooked *N* that had been written on it in bright green glitter paint had Alyssa smiling, knowing it had been made with love.

She did one final walk-through of the house to make sure everything looked just right. Snowman placemats surrounded a centerpiece done in silver and blue ribbon with a coating of fake snow dusted over it. A porcelain nativity scene sat atop a gold table runner on the coffee table. Snowflakes she and Katie had cut out of paper Alyssa had brought with her hung in all the front windows upstairs and downstairs. A pair of holiday hand towels hung from the wooden towel bar on the downstairs half bath wall. Outside on the porch, a large wreath hung on the front door. Below it, a welcome mat designed to look like a gift with Welcome printed on its tag awaited holiday visitors.

She couldn't wait for Nathan to get home and see it all. The thought had no sooner crossed her mind than she heard his truck coming up the drive. She hurried to Katie's room, giving her a gentle shake. "Your daddy's home."

Katie shot upright in her bed. Sleep clearing quickly from her eyes, replaced by unrestrained excitement. "He is?"

"Yes," she told her. "We'll greet him at the door when he comes in."

Katie sprung out of bed.

Together, they hurried down the stairs to welcome Nathan home.

Stepping up to the front window, Alyssa peeked outside. Sure enough, his truck sat in the drive. Turning away from the window with a soft giggle, she moved to stand behind Katie, her hands clasped over her tiny shoulders.

The thump of booted footsteps sounded on the front porch.

"He's coming," Katie whispered.

"I know." Reaching out, Alyssa flipped the light switch that would turn on the outside lights that she and Katie had hung along the porch rail and around the front door. Her heart pounded with excitement as she waited for Nathan to step inside, a smile on his handsome face.

Only the door didn't open.

"Where is Daddy?" Katie said, her voice hushed.

Alyssa glanced toward the window, wondering herself what was taking him so long. Had Nathan forgotten something in his truck? No, she would have heard him move back across the porch. Maybe he'd gotten a call and was finishing it up before coming inside.

Then the doorknob rattled, the front door swinging open to reveal Nathan's tall form. Only he wasn't smiling. His face looked as if it were carved out of granite, his jaw was clenched so tight.

"Surprise!" Katie exclaimed before Alyssa had a chance to stop her. It was just as they'd planned, only something was wrong.

"Nathan?" she said, trying to get a feel for what was going on with him.

"What did you do?" he demanded, his voice tight. Not with emotion but with something else. Anger?

"Katie and I wanted to surprise you," she said, forcing a smile.

"Well, you succeeded," he said with a frown as his gaze swept the inside of the house. His expression hardened even more. "Katie, go to your room."

"But I just came down," she whined.

"Miss McCall and I need to talk. Go."

"It's okay, sweetie," Alyssa assured her. "It won't take long." As soon as she had disappeared up the stairs, she turned back to Nathan. "What is going on with you?"

"*You* had no right to do this!" he said, motioning around him.

"I thought that since you didn't have time to decorate for Christmas, Katie and I could do it for you."

"Time had nothing to do with my not putting up decorations," he said through clenched teeth. "I don't want festive lights and smiling snowmen filling my house. I don't want any reminders of what the holidays mean to me. The loss of my wife. Of Katie's mother. Of my parents. Of the life I was supposed to be living!"

She reached for him, tears in her eyes. "Oh, Nathan, I'm so sorry."

He pulled away. "Don't. I can't do this. Not right now." Turning away, he walked back out the door.

She went after him, standing in the doorway as he strode toward his truck. "Where are you going?"

"I need to clear my head," he shot back as he moved in angry strides around to the driver's side. And then, he was gone.

# Chapter Twelve

"It's all my fault."

Alyssa turned to see Katie standing at the foot of the stairs, her favorite princess doll clutched to her chest, tears rolling down her cheeks. "Oh, honey, nothing is your fault."

"Yes, it is. My daddy's mad at you and it's all my fault. I showed you where the Christmas boxes were."

"He's not mad at me," she said, trying to calm Katie. "He was just...surprised." Only not in the way they'd intended him to be.

Katie shook her head with a sob. "I heard him yell at you. Now you'll never get to be my mommy, and my daddy will go back to being sad again."

Before she could respond, Katie ran off toward the kitchen. A door slammed, making Alyssa gasp. "Katie!" she hollered as she raced into the kitchen. The blinds hanging over the back door window were swinging to and fro. Katie had gone outside.

The poor thing was so upset and she couldn't blame her. Alyssa followed her outside, expecting to find her sitting on one of the porch chairs, but she was nowhere to be seen.

"Katie?" she called out, trying to remain calm despite her pounding heart. "Where are you?"

When she didn't answer, Alyssa ran back into the house to grab her cell phone and Katie's coat before hurrying back outside. Still no sign of her. She called Nathan, but his phone went straight to voice mail. So she called Audra.

"Hello?"

"Audra, it's Alyssa," she said, trying to calm her breathing. "Do you know where Nathan is by any chance?"

"No, I don't," she replied. "You sound upset. Is everything all right?"

Alyssa fought back the tears. "No, it's not. Nathan left and I can't reach him. Katie ran off somewhere and I can't find her. And it's getting dark."

"I'm sure she's fine. Just calm down and tell me what happened."

"There's no time," she replied. "I have to find Katie." Disconnecting the call, she started across the yard, calling out to Katie as she went.

When she reached the pines that lined the expansive backyard, Alyssa caught sight of something shimmering in the fading light and moved toward it.

Katie's princess doll, with its sparkly gown and miniature tiara, lay face down on the bed of pine needles that covered the forest floor. She picked it up and looked around. "Katie!"

The woods were cast in shadows and would only grow darker as the sun dipped beneath the distant horizon. She stepped through the wall of pines, holding Katie's coat up in front of her face to shield her eyes as she went. Thankfully, the woods thinned out and she was able to move more freely through them.

An owl screeched somewhere in the treetops above her, making Alyssa jump. She had grown up in cities, not somewhere wild animals roamed free. She knew about traversing sidewalks, not finding her way through thickly wooded acreage.

"Katie!" she called out louder, her desperation growing. It felt like she'd been walking forever. *Please, Lord, keep her safe in Your loving arms until I can find her.*

The cell phone she clutched in her hand rang. She'd forgotten she held it. "Hello," she said, her hand trembling as she held it to her ear.

The caller's voice on the other end was garbled, cutting in and out. She glanced down at the screen. It was Carter. "If you can hear me, I'm in the woods behind the house, searching for Katie. Please tell Nathan I need him." The call cut out before she could say anything more.

Alyssa's gaze swept the thickening shadows and a feeling of helplessness came over her. Her vision was blurred. How would she ever find Katie when she could barely see the trees in front of her? Was she even searching for her in the right area? She'd wandered so deep into the woods she wasn't even certain where she was herself or if she'd be able to find her way out. All that mattered was finding Katie. Poor, sweet, heartbroken Katie.

Why had she ever allowed herself to believe she could be the woman to make Nathan happy? And now, under her care, Katie had run off into the woods alone. She had failed Nathan. And now she was failing Katie.

She struggled onward, another spindly branch clawing at her face and snagging the sleeve of her sweater. She felt a trickle of warmth slide down her scratched cheek. Tears welled up in her eyes. She turned the screen of her phone on, hoping to try to reach Nathan again, but there was no signal now whatsoever. Distracted, she didn't see the gnarled root protruding from the forest floor. She went down hard, landing on her knees. Katie's coat cushioned the ground beneath her hands, but the impact sent her phone skittering out of her hand to disappear into the blur of the woods around her.

She struggled to find it, her hand sweeping frantically over the ground around her until she felt its familiar shape beneath her fingers. Then, clutching tightly to the phone, she shifted into a sitting position and tipped her face upward. Her gaze fixed on the blur of treetops and the fading sky above, she offered up a silent prayer.

She was still sitting there when the rain began to fall in thick, cold drops. Her tears quickly followed, turning into loud, wrenching sobs as the feeling of true helplessness overcame her.

"Alyssa?" a fearful voice called out in the distance.

Her head snapped around. "Katie!" she gasped, between sobs. Relief swept through her. Katie was safe. She scrambled to her feet. "Stay where you are," she hollered back. "I'll come to you. Just keep talking."

"I don't like the dark," Katie cried out.

"We'll be home before you know it," she called out reassuringly as she followed the sound of Katie's voice deeper into the woods.

"I'm sorry I ran away," she heard her say.

"I know you are, sweetie." All that mattered was that she was safe. "Can you see me yet?"

"Y-yes."

She had to be close or she wouldn't have been able to make out the sound of Katie's teeth chattering. "You can come to me now, Katie." She held out her arms, desperate to hold Katie in them. To know that she truly was safe. If anything had happened to her... She couldn't even bear to think of what it would do to Nathan.

Tiny feet shuffled across the ground and then slender arms wrapped around Alyssa's waist in a fierce hold. Katie sniffled softly. "I'm so glad you came looking for me."

"Of course I came looking for you," she said as she wrapped her arms around the trembling little girl beside her. "I love you, sweetie." And she did. Every bit as much as she loved her daddy.

Katie looked up at her, drops of rain stinging her face. "I love you, too, Alyssa."

"I have something that belongs to you." She held up the dirty, wet doll.

"Is that Princess Sparkles?"

"It sure is." She handed the wet doll into Katie's safekeeping. "We took a bit of a tumble, but we can clean her up once when we get home."

"She's missing her crown," she said worriedly.

"We'll find it, sweetie. We might just have to wait until tomorrow when there's more light to see by."

"Okay." Katie shivered. "This rain is making Princess Sparkles cold."

"Then you'll have to tuck her inside your coat to keep her warm," Alyssa told her as she held the blessedly well-insulated, waterproof jacket out for Katie to slide her arms into it. Thankfully, she'd thought to grab it on her way out the door. If only she'd thought to grab her own, as well. But then she hadn't intended to venture into the woods when she'd left the house in search of Katie. She knelt on a bruised knee to zip Katie up snuggly. "Better?"

She nodded. "Princess Sparkles is happy." Then she frowned. "Where's your coat?"

Alyssa gave her a reassuring smile as she straightened, knees aching. "We'll be home long before I need it." At least, she prayed they would be. Surely, someone would find them soon. Instinct had her wanting to get Katie back to the safety of her home, but common sense reminded her that when lost in the woods, it was best to stay in one place and wait for help to arrive rather than risk getting even more lost.

Taking Katie's hand in hers, she looked around. "We need to find a dry place to wait for your daddy." *Dear Lord, please let him find us soon.* Crawling under the thick bushes beside them was their best option. It wouldn't keep out all the rain, but it was better than where they were standing now.

"We could wait in the cave."

Alyssa looked down at her. "What cave?"

"The one I found back there," she said, pointing in the direction from which she'd come. "But it's dark."

"Dark is better than cold and wet," she told her. "Do you think you can find it for us?"

She nodded, her wet curls drooping down over her damp face. "This way," she said, tugging at Alyssa's hand. Not more than thirty feet ahead the thickening of pines opened up onto a rocky hillside. Katie led her around to the far side where she pointed to a wide crevice in the rocks. "There it is."

The opening was probably a good eight feet wide and maybe five feet tall at its highest point. Inside it was dark. Who knew what else huddled in there for protection from the cold and the rain?

"Stay here a minute while I have a look inside." Pulling her cell phone from the back pocket of her jeans, she tapped on the flashlight icon. A beam of light streamed from the back of the phone, lighting the cave's entrance. She stepped closer, listening for any sound of movement. Hard to tell with the rain coming down outside, but surely if something was in there it would have tried to flee when it heard them approaching from the woods.

Movement on the floor in front of her drew her gaze down to what looked to be a very large centipede. At least eight inches in length. She took a step back with a shudder, waiting until it had disappeared from sight before venturing farther into the cave. Raising the light, she cringed when she saw a gossamer web stretched across a portion of the cave's ceiling to one side. She was quite certain the blur she saw in it was a spider waiting patiently for its next meal. Other than those two creatures, the cave appeared to be a safe haven from the elements outside.

"Come on in, sweetie," she called out.

"Are there bats in here?" Katie asked as she took a tentative step inside.

"Not that I see. Just a wonderfully creative spider adding a touch of decor to our temporary rain shelter."

Katie seemed to be satisfied with that answer, moving farther in to where Alyssa stood to admire the spider's handiwork for herself. "It's pretty."

She would have to take Katie's word for it as the finer details of the web were lost to her. "Let's have a seat while we wait."

They settled onto the dirt floor, Katie safely ensconced in Alyssa's lap. She wrapped her arms around both Katie and her beloved doll, her heart aching. She'd come so close to having a family of her own, but tonight had proved she could never be anybody's mother. A tear rolled down her cheek, the saltiness of it stinging the scratches on her face.

"What do we do now?" Katie asked.

"We say a prayer of thanks to God for providing us with shelter when we needed it," Alyssa said as her gaze fell to the cell phone she held clenched in her hand. Prayer appeared to be their only hope as a cell signal was nonexistent.

Together they bowed their heads and prayed. Then Alyssa pressed a kiss to Katie's rain-dampened hair. "Now close your eyes and try to get some sleep."

Katie curled up against her, the warmth of her tiny body helping to ease some of the cold that had seeped into Alyssa's bones as she'd walked coatless through the rain. "Will you tell me a story?"

Alyssa smiled softly, her heart so full of love for this little girl. "It would be my pleasure." Resting her chin atop Katie's head, she began, "Once upon a time there was a beautiful princess…"

Rain splattered across the windshield as the storm the weather station had predicted moved in. Having driven around the back roads of Braxton for a good hour or so, the shock and pain he'd felt when he'd first arrived home that evening had faded. In its place, guilt washed over him.

He could still see the confusion and hurt on Alyssa's face when he'd allowed his pain to loosen his tongue. She'd had only good intentions and he'd blamed her for something she had no way of knowing would upset him. He'd never told her about his aversion to all things Christmas. And if his behavior toward Alyssa hadn't been bad enough, he'd raised his voice to his daughter, something he'd never done. She'd been so excited for him to see what they'd done while he was at work. But once he'd seen that wreath hanging on the front door, the one his wife had made just days before the tornado struck, he'd been overwhelmed by emotions he didn't want to feel.

Needing just a few more moments to process his thoughts before returning home, he pulled off on the side of the road and cut the engine. Then he let his head drop back against the headrest and closed his eyes.

He owed Alyssa an apology. Now that he'd had time to recover from the shock of coming home to a house filled with holiday cheer, he knew that he'd been wrong to take the joy of Christmas away from his daughter. To take away the memories Isabel would have wanted him to share with their daughter.

Like Alyssa, his wife had taken great delight in the holidays. In the true meaning of Christmas. In the Lord. She believed Christmas was a time to receive God's tender mercy, abundant love, forgiveness and grace.

Maybe it was time for him to let go of the anger he'd been holding on to, which had left him feeling cold and empty, and step willingly back into the Lord's embrace.

A horn blasted on the road behind him. Nathan opened his eyes just as Carter pulled up alongside his truck, motioning for him to lower his window. He did despite the rain, the expression on his brother's face telling him something had happened. Nathan's gut clenched.

"Where have you been?" his brother demanded.

"Took a few back roads before parking to mull a few things over. Why? What's wrong?"

"You need to get home. Now," his brother said with an urgency that had Nathan's heart dropping.

"Is it Katie?" he asked, barely managing to get the words out.

His brother nodded. "She ran off and Alyssa is out in the woods looking for her."

"In the woods?" he exclaimed. Katie never went any farther than the end of their yard.

"That's what Alyssa told me before the call cut out," his brother replied as the rain fell harder.

"She'd have little or no signal in those woods," Nathan called out over the pounding rain. Then his brother's words hit him like a blow to the gut. "Alyssa called you?" Had he messed things up so badly between them that she'd sought help from his brother instead of him in her time of need?

"She tried to reach you," he yelled out, "but it went straight to voice mail. So she called Audra, who called me."

"How long ago?" he said as he started his truck.

"Not quite an hour ago. I was in Uvalde picking up some supplies when Audra called to tell me what happened. That's where I'm coming from now. Logan should already be at the house."

With a nod, Nathan threw the truck into gear and hit the gas. His girls needed him. His gaze penetrated the rain outside to settle on the dense woods that covered his property. The sun, barely visible behind the thick, gray clouds, was rapidly setting behind the distant mountains for the night. The woods would be dark, cast in shadows. And, in this rain, damp and bitingly cold. Katie and Alyssa were out there alone, and it was all his fault.

Nathan knew what he had to do. Something he hadn't done for two long years. He prayed. "Lord, I humbly ask for Your forgiveness for turning my back on You during my time of loss. I was weak and I lost my way. In Your good grace, You sent Alyssa into my life. A woman strong in her faith and convictions, a woman blessed with a giving heart. Through *Your* love and her gentle patience, I am finding my way back. I pray that You will watch over my daughter and the woman I love, keeping them safe until they can be found. Amen."

Logan's truck sat in the driveway in front of the house when they arrived. Nathan parked his truck and jumped out. Carter did the same.

"We'll need flashlights," he told Nathan.

He raced into the house to grab a battery-operated spotlight and a couple of flashlights along with a pair of two-way radios.

Carter met him out back. "Got everything?"

Nathan nodded, handing his brother a flashlight. "Let's go." They set off in a jog across the rain-slickened yard and were almost to the tree line when Logan stepped from the woods.

Hope flared inside Nathan for the briefest moment. Then his gaze moved past his brother to see that no one followed him out. He met Logan's gaze. "No sign of them?"

Logan shook his head. "I picked up a trail and was able to follow it about a hundred yards in, but it got too dark to see."

Nathan handed him the other flashlight and then turned on the battery-operated spotlight he'd brought along. "Let's go find my girls."

Logan led them back to the trail he'd been following. "What do you think happened?" he asked, his voice raised over the sound of the rain. "It's not like Katie to run off like this."

The guilt returned full force. "*I* happened," Nathan admitted. "The girls thought they'd surprise me by bringing out the Christmas decorations. Katie was so excited. Alyssa had a smile on her beautiful face." He looked to his brothers. "And I raised my voice to them both, told them they had no right to do what they'd done, then I walked out."

His brothers looked his way, concern filling their eyes.

"I need to find them," he said brokenly. "Need to tell them how sorry I am and ask for their forgiveness."

"Don't worry. We'll find them," Carter said.

Despite his brothers' assurances, they soon discovered that any trail left behind by Alyssa and his daughter was quickly being washed away by the rain. At least Alyssa was moving in the same direction that Katie had gone in. He had to wonder if God hadn't had a hand in that, considering Alyssa's limited vision. He said a silent prayer of thanks to the Lord for guiding them down the same path and asked that He continue to keep them safe from harm.

They'd gone nearly three-quarters of a mile into the woods, calling out to Katie and Alyssa in hopes of getting some sort of verbal response. But the only sound came from the rain falling through the trees to the ground below.

"How can they not hear us?" Nathan said in frustration. "Voice carries in the night."

"The rain probably isn't helping matters," Carter acknowledged as he raised the collar of his coat in an effort to keep out the pulsing rain.

"I reckon it's possible we're following the wrong trail," Logan suggested with a frown. "With all this rain and the lack of good light, it's hard to tell if the tracks we're picking up around here now are animal or human."

"They're human," Carter said from where he searched about ten feet away.

They turned their lights onto him to see their brother holding up a small, glittery crown.

Nathan closed the distance between himself and Carter and reached for the silvery piece. "That's Princess Sparkles's crown."

Logan motioned to the ground. "Looks like someone fell."

Nathan's first thought was that it had been Katie who had fallen. How else would her doll's crown have ended up on the ground? He clutched the tiny crown in the palm of his hand, his gut clenching as he looked to the spot his brother was pointing out. Sure enough there were two deep indents in the soft earth where what he assumed had to be knees had dug in. Just past the pitted ground, the bed of pine needles that made up the forest floor had been tunneled through in two long lines. Too big to have been made by Katie's hands.

"Alyssa," he said, his words barely audible. His light shone on the gnarled root sticking up only a couple feet away. Of course, she wouldn't have seen it. Not with her poor vision and the fading light of day. Had she injured herself in the fall? And was Katie with her now? She had to be, he told himself. How else would that crown have gotten there? Alyssa had found his daughter.

Carter clasped a hand over Nathan's shoulder. "There's no blood, and the fall didn't keep her from continuing on. That's a good sign."

Nathan's frown deepened. "Except that they're going in the wrong direction."

"Unless they respond soon to our hollering,

we're gonna lose their trail altogether. The rain's coming down too hard," Logan said, unable to keep the urgency from his voice.

"No, we're not," Carter said, drawing both men's worried gazes his way. "Boone can find them."

Boone was the droopy-faced bloodhound mix Carter and Audra had adopted from the pound for the kids. Despite his massive size, weighing in now at close to eighty pounds, the dog still hadn't reached full maturity. He still liked to test the limits Carter set for him. But Nathan was willing to try whatever it took to find Katie and Alyssa. If they didn't find them soon, he was calling the sheriff to start a search party.

He looked to Carter and said determinedly. "Get him. Logan and I will keep looking."

With a nod, Carter took off through the woods, dodging back and forth around trees and brush until he'd disappeared behind a curtain of darkness and rain.

"Katie!" Nathan hollered again, his voice starting to show the strain of the repeated yelling he'd done.

"Alyssa!" his brother joined in, his voice sounding no better.

Still no response.

He would not allow his thoughts to travel down a negative path. He would trust in God's will and hope that *His* will was for them to bring Katie and Alyssa home safely. Nathan turned to his brother. "Before we go any farther, there's something I'd like for us to do."

"Name it," Logan said.

"I'd like for us to pray."

Something wet moved over Alyssa's cheek. She swatted at it sleepily. Then as the memory of the huge centipede she'd seen crossing the cave floor came into her groggy mind, her eyes shot open. Something warm and moist caressed her face.

*Dear Lord, please don't let it be a bear.*

Lifting her phone with trembling hands, her heart pounding, Alyssa turned on the flashlight. Two dark eyes surrounded by sagging folds of fur-covered skin peered into her face. Try as she might, she couldn't keep the startled shriek from escaping her lips.

Katie's head shot up, awakened from the peaceful slumber she'd fallen into. The squeal she let out put Alyssa's to shame. "Boone!"

Before Alyssa could stop her, Katie flew at the bear, throwing her arms around its neck. Horrified, Alyssa moved to pull her back and put herself between Katie and the whimpering bear.

"Oh, Boone, you found us," Katie was saying. "Good dog."

*Good dog?* The giant creature was a dog? Alyssa felt light-headed with relief.

"Boone!" a familiar voice called out from the darkness outside.

The dog barked in response.

"Uncle Carter!" Katie exclaimed.

"Katydid?"

"Katie!" Nathan's worried voice carried into the cave.

"We're in here!" Alyssa called out, shining the beam of light from her phone out into the night.

Footsteps pounded atop the muddied ground outside, coming closer. A moment later, three hulking figures squeezed into the opening of the cave.

"Daddy!" Katie shot out of Alyssa's lap, running toward him.

Setting the light he held down beside him, he knelt on the ground, catching Katie in his outstretched arms. He hugged her tight, pressing kisses to the top of her tiny head. "Baby girl," he said, holding her away from him to look her over. "Are you all right?"

She nodded. "I was scared, but Alyssa found me."

He looked past Katie to where Alyssa sat unmoving on the floor of the cave. "Logan," he called back over his shoulder.

"I've got her," his brother said, reaching for Katie.

"I'm gonna take Boone outside," Carter said as he clipped a leash onto the dog's collar.

"We're right behind you," Logan said, bending low as he carried Katie out of the cave.

Tears rolled down Alyssa's cheeks. *Katie was safe. Katie was safe.* That was all she could think about as she sat shivering on the ground.

Then Nathan was there, wrapping his strong arms around her. "Alyssa."

She leaned into his warmth, trembling.

He immediately pulled away, his gaze moving over her. "Where's your coat?"

"B-back at the house."

"But Katie had hers on," he said, as he hurried to remove his own coat.

"I grabbed it when I went in to get my phone," she said as he worked her chilled arms through its sleeves.

"And not your own?" he said as he bundled her up in the warmth of his coat.

"There wasn't time."

Reaching up, he pushed the tangle of her hair back from her face and gasped. "You're hurt."

"A few scratches."

Cupping her chin he tipped her face upward

to inspect it. "Your beautiful face," he said, his words filled with anguish. Then, leaning forward, he pressed a tender kiss to her cheek. "Thank you for being there for my daughter and keeping her safe."

"We were there for each other," she said, her voice cracking. "And your thanks should go to the Lord who kept us safe and gave us shelter."

"I agree," he said, his response surprising her. "God is good. He answered my prayers."

She lifted her head to look up at him. "You prayed?"

He nodded. "God and I had a long talk. Actually, I did all the talking, but that's how it needed to be. I asked for His forgiveness and then asked that He bring you and Katie home safe to me. My prayers were answered." Lifting her into his arms, he stood, leaning forward just enough to avoid the cave's low ceiling. "Time to go home."

Tears filled her eyes as he carried her out to where the others waited. Just when Nathan finally found his way back to the Lord, something she needed for their relationship to work, her own failings made it clear she could never be a part of his life the way she'd hoped to be. No matter how deeply she loved him.

## Chapter Thirteen

"Gather up your things, Cupcake. We've got a few errands to run before we head to the rec center this morning."

"Okay!" Katie exclaimed, excited to be well enough to be around other people again. She scurried off to her bedroom to get her backpack full of coloring books and crayons and the handheld gaming system Nathan's brothers had bought her last Christmas.

He'd called Alyssa after Logan had taken her home the night before, needing to hear her voice. Needing to know that she was okay after all that had transpired, since they'd had little time to talk when they'd gotten back to the house the night before. All focus had been on tending to Alyssa's injuries and warming her and Katie by the fire. When Alyssa'd asked Logan to take her back to the boardinghouse,

Nathan had insisted he take her. She'd refused, telling him that his place was with his daughter. But there was so much he'd wanted to say to her. Words that would just have to wait until the time was right. So he'd settled for another heartfelt thank-you and then told her to sleep in. That he and Katie would pick her up around eleven the following morning to take her to see the newly completed rec center.

Smiling, Nathan walked into the kitchen to grab his coat from its hook by the door. He couldn't wait for Alyssa to see all her design plans in their finished state. She was as much a part of this project as he and his brothers were and she'd missed so much staying home with Katie. Everything fit so well, from the colors she'd chosen for each room to the various types of flooring that had needed to be laid. Even the furniture, a more modern style than he would have chosen, worked perfectly.

Rusty Clark, representing the town council, had stopped by the rec center the previous afternoon and had been duly impressed by the detail Alyssa had put into the project. He'd even placed a call to the design firm she worked for, putting in a word of praise for her work. Not that it mattered, Nathan thought to himself, his smile widening. If everything worked out as he hoped it would, this would be just the first of

many projects he and Alyssa would be working on together. Her firm hadn't realized what
a true talent Alyssa still was, but he did.

Pulling out his cell, he called Carter.

"Are you at the rec center?"

"Got here about twenty minutes ago," Carter
replied. "Logan is in the gymnasium, making
sure the Christmas tree is secure before it's decorated. The crew and I are packing away the
rest of our tools. Then I'm sending them home
to their families. You on your way in or is my
little Katydid still sleeping?"

"Are you kidding? She was up hours ago. She
can't wait to see the rec center."

"She'll be surprised."

"That she will." So much had changed during the time Katie had been forced to stay home
while she recuperated from chicken pox. "The
reason I'm calling is to ask you for a favor."

"Name it," his brother said without hesitation.

"Katie and I have a couple of special errands
we need to see to in town. She wants to get
Alyssa something special to thank her for what
she did."

"A nice gesture," Carter agreed. "But then
my niece did inherit her thoughtfulness from
me. What's the other errand?"

Nathan smiled. "I wanted to get Alyssa something special, as well. She's expecting Katie and

me to pick her up around eleven, but I'm not sure if we'll be done in time. Think you can run out to the boardinghouse and pick her up around that time?"

"I'd be glad to."

"Thanks, Carter. I owe you one." Disconnecting the call, he went to round up his daughter.

A little over an hour later, he and Katie pulled into the rec center parking lot. Carter hadn't returned yet from picking up Alyssa. That was good. It gave him time to collect himself and go over the words he wanted to say in his head before he actually tried to speak them.

"Everything looks so pretty," his daughter exclaimed the second they stepped through the door.

Nathan smiled, understanding her surprise over what had been done. She hadn't seen the rec center since coming down with chicken pox. "Alyssa did a fine job."

"With my help," Katie promptly reminded him.

He chuckled. "That goes without saying, Cupcake." He ruffled her dark curls playfully. "Daddy's very proud of the work you and Alyssa did here."

She looked up at him. "Do you think Alyssa is mad at us?"

Her words brought forth the same concern

that had plagued him through the night. Not in regards to Alyssa being upset with Katie. He knew better. Alyssa understood why Katie had reacted the way she had. But a part of him worried that his apology hadn't taken all the sting of his words away. Hopefully, his intended surprise would stir her to forgive him and allow them to become the family he knew they could be.

"No, honey," he replied with confidence. "She's not mad at us. Why would you think that?"

She looked down at the toe of her boots. "'Cause you yelled at her and I ran away and made her get hurt."

He smiled reassuringly. "She understands that everybody has a bad day once in a while and that Daddy is very sorry for raising his voice to the both of you." At least, he hoped she did. But he left his explanation at that, since Katie wasn't quite old enough to understand the emotions that had driven him to react the way he had. "And Alyssa doesn't blame you for her getting hurt. She loves you. So much so, she went into the woods to find you, even though her eyes aren't able to see as good as most people's. That's why she fell. She didn't see the root sticking up through the fallen pine needles."

"I love her, too," his daughter said.

"That makes two of us," he told her.

Her eyes widened. "Even without the mistletoe?"

His brows furrowed in confusion. "Mistletoe?"

She nodded. "Remember what Alyssa told us in the toy store? She said mistletoe makes people kiss and fall in love. But you had to be standing under it for it to work." She looked up at him. "Is there mistletoe in our woods?"

He chuckled. "Not that I know of. Sometimes the heart just knows, even without the help of mistletoe."

The rec center door swung open and Carter stepped inside—alone.

"Where's Alyssa?" Nathan asked.

"She's not coming in," Carter said, frowning.

"What do you mean she's not coming in?"

"Does she have my chicken pox?" Katie asked worriedly.

"No, honey," Carter said. "She doesn't have your chicken pox. As far as I could tell, she wasn't sick at all. Just a little out of sorts."

"Cupcake," Nathan said, his gaze fixed on his brother, "Daddy needs to have a word in private with Uncle Carter. Why don't you take your backpack into the art room and draw Alyssa a pretty picture to give her with the flowers we picked up for her?"

Carter nodded. "I'll bet she'd like that."

"Okay," she said, walking over to grab her backpack off one of the lobby chairs.

Nathan waited until she was out of hearing before saying, "Are you certain she's not sick? They were out in that damp weather for nearly three hours last night."

"I reckon she could be, but her coloring looked good," Carter replied. "But she seemed a bit off."

"Off how?"

His brother shrugged. "Not real sure how to explain it. Withdrawn, maybe. I suppose she might just be a little skittish after all that happened yesterday. What she went through had to have worn on her mentally. Probably why she said she needed some time to sort through things today."

Concern coming over his face, Nathan pulled his phone from the front pocket of his jeans. This was not a good sign.

"I think I'd wait on calling her," his brother suggested with an empathetic smile. "When a woman asks for some time to herself, a smart man knows to steer clear. Take it from a man who was in the not-so-smart category where Audra was concerned during one of our earlier rough patches."

It took everything in him to hold off on calling Alyssa. He needed to know where her head was at. And, more importantly, where her heart was. Because he knew how he felt. He loved her. Couldn't imagine his life without her in it. But his brother was right. She'd been through an ordeal yesterday, and he needed to respect her need for some breathing room.

Until then, he needed to try to redirect his thoughts elsewhere. "Let's get this place cleaned up." All that was left to haul out to their trucks were a couple of nail guns they'd used for the trim and baseboards, a table saw, a scattering of hand tools and the plywood and sawhorses they had set up to do the final cuts on the trim.

Carter looked around the room. "Hard to believe this place is gonna be all festive and filled with townsfolk in a few days."

Nathan nodded. It was even harder to believe that he was going to be there attending the Christmas Eve gathering along with them. But he would be. Not only for Katie's sake, but for the woman he loved. Alyssa loved the holidays, something she'd never had the chance to enjoy growing up. He wanted to be the man to give her all those things she'd missed out on. A real home. A family. Love.

"I'm gonna ask Alyssa to marry me."

Carter's head snapped around, his eyes wide. "Run that by me again."

"I love her," he admitted aloud for the first time. It felt good. "And before you try to talk me out of rushing into things—"

"Hold up a moment, big brother," Carter said with a grin. "Remember who you're talking to. It's not like I took my time getting to the altar once I knew Audra was the one for me."

His brother's response lightening his mood, Nathan chuckled. "How do you think Logan's gonna react to the news?"

"After what Alyssa did for Katie last night, I wouldn't be surprised if he was thinking about marrying her himself."

That wiped the smile from Nathan's face.

This time it was Carter who was chuckling aloud. "Boy, do you have it bad. Question for you, big brother. Have you told Alyssa yet that you love her?"

"Not in those exact words," he admitted.

"Might be good to get that little tidbit in before you actually propose to her. Take it from a man who knows."

It was all Alyssa could do to force herself from bed that morning, only a few days shy of what would have been her first Christmas Eve with Nathan and Katie. Even a call from her design firm, telling her they wanted to discuss bringing her back on full-time when she returned to San Antonio hadn't lifted her spirits.

She'd dressed, her heart heavy, knowing Nathan and Katie would be by to pick her up to go tour the newly completed recreation center. Knowing she wouldn't be going with them. But Carter had shown up in their place, telling her Nathan had a few things he'd needed to take care of in town and would meet them at the rec center. Probably a blessing. She wasn't certain she was strong enough yet to do what she had to do. Instead, she had sent Carter on his way, telling him she needed some time to herself.

Her work at the recreation center was done. It was time to go. Even if her heart was pleading with her to stay. All she wanted to do was go back to bed and pull the covers up over her head and cry some more. Just as she had all night. But that wouldn't change anything. Her visual impairment had put Katie's life at risk. What if next time Katie wasn't physically able to cry out for help so Alyssa could find her? She shuddered at the thought of what that could have meant for Katie.

No, Katie deserved a mother who could protect her from harm. And Nathan deserved a woman he could trust to keep his daughter safe. She wasn't that woman.

Tears spilled down her cheeks as she pulled

her suitcase from the closet and placed it atop the bed. Then she reached toward the nightstand for her cell phone and dialed Erica's number.

"Good morning!" her best friend chirped when she answered.

Oh, how she wished it were. But there was nothing good about having to walk away from the man that you loved.

"Alyssa?"

"Can you come get me?"

"I thought you were gonna be staying in Braxton through the holidays."

"Things have changed," she said, her voice catching.

"I hate that Nathan hurt you."

"I'm the one who is gonna be hurting him," she said, her heart breaking at the thought of it. "But sometimes when you truly love someone, you have to set them free."

"Did you say *love*? As in you're in *love* with Nathan?"

"And his precious little girl," Alyssa replied, tears filling her eyes.

"Alyssa," her friend said, her tone laced with a mix of compassion and concern. "You love him. Whyever would you feel the need to walk away?"

With a heavy sigh, she went on to tell her friend all that had happened the night before.

Then she hung up and started packing her things. Erica had tried to convince her to rethink her decision, but Alyssa knew it would be selfish of her to stay. So she was doing the only other thing she could. She was going home.

By the time she'd finished packing, exhaustion, both mental and physical, had her crawling back atop the quilted bedspread and closing her eyes. She had a few hours before Erica could get there to pick her up and even less time before she had to face Nathan with the news of her leaving. But for now, all she wanted to do was sleep. And so she did.

A tap at the bedroom door roused Alyssa from sleep. "Come in," she said tiredly.

Doris poked her head in the door, announcing in that sweet, grandmotherly voice Alyssa recognized immediately, "You have a visitor, dear."

A visitor? Sitting up, she swung her legs off the bed. "I'll be right down," she told her as the sleep cleared from her mind.

"No need," the older woman said. "He's right here. I'll give you two a moment to talk while I go put the teapot on."

Doris scurried off and a very tall, slightly blurred form stepped in from the hallway. The second her vision adjusted enough to see her visitor somewhat clearly, she gasped. "Nathan?"

He moved toward her, a frown on his face. "Never took you for a quitter."

Her heart lurched.

"Or is Erica mistaken about your leaving town?"

"How did you—"

"She called me," he said, his hurt at what she'd intended to do clear in his voice.

She pushed off the bed and walked over to look out the window, unable to face him. "She shouldn't have."

He stepped forward, boots clicking across the hardwood floor as he closed the distance between them. His hands came to rest on her shoulders, gently turning her to face him. "Were you really gonna leave without saying good-bye?"

She forced herself to meet his troubled gaze, guilt filling her. "No," she said in a whisper. "I would have said goodbye."

"What about Katie?" he asked. "You're gonna break her heart."

"I have to go," she said with a soft sob. "She could have died last night because of me."

"But she didn't," he said determinedly, running his hands up and down her arms in a slow, calming manner.

"I couldn't even get her back home once we found each other," she said with a soft sob.

"Grown men have gotten turned around in those woods in broad daylight. And you never gave up on finding her, despite the dark, despite the cold, despite the miserable rain."

Her bottom lip quivered as she fought to hold back the tears. "She's better off without me."

"I'm not so sure she'd agree," he replied. "I know I don't."

"Nathan…"

"Alyssa, *you* are the one we want in our lives. *You* are the one I trust to care for my daughter."

"How can you trust me to care for her after last night?"

He smiled tenderly. "You've nursed my daughter through a lengthy illness, caring for her as if she were your very own. And when my thoughtless words sent her running in tears from the house, you didn't allow your visual limitations to keep you from going after her." He reached out to gently brush his thumb over her tender cheek. "You risked and endured injury to find her. And once you did, you made certain Katie was warm and protected until we could find you both." He let his hand fall away. "How could I not trust you?"

Tears spilled down her cheeks. His kind words, his gentle touch, were weakening her already shaky resolve.

"Say you'll at least stay until the party," he

pleaded. "For Katie's sake. She's expecting you to be there and she's not the only one," he reminded her. "Rusty and his wife, the reverend, my brothers, Audra and her little ones, the ladies from the church. I could go on and on."

Her gaze settled onto the hardwood floor between them. "I don't know if I can."

"Reckon that makes two of us."

She looked up at him questioningly.

"For the first time in two years, I'll be taking part in the town's Christmas Eve celebration. That means surrounding myself with all that warm, fuzzy holiday cheer I've been so determined to steer clear of. And then there's the dedication. It's not gonna be easy," he said, his words taut with emotion. "I don't wanna do this alone."

"Nathan…"

"You are my heart's light, Alyssa. Say you'll go with me and help to keep the darkness away."

"Tea's ready," Doris interrupted from the doorway. "Why don't you kids come on down to the parlor and have some? Myrna made coffee cake this morning. You can have some of it with your tea while you two sweethearts make up."

*Make up?* Before Alyssa could set Doris straight on her misconception that there could be anything more than friendship between her and Nathan, the older woman was gone.

Nathan released her, letting his hands fall away. "What do you say, darlin'? You willing to sit down with me and talk things through?"

"It won't change anything," she told him as she reached for her suitcase. "I'm not meant to be in your lives." No matter how desperately she wished it to be true.

Just like the first day they met, his hand beat hers to the handle of her suitcase, curling firmly around it. "I've got it."

"You don't have to—"

"Seems to me we've had this conversation before," he said as he headed toward the open door. Stopping in the doorway, he turned to her with a grin the size of Texas. "As far as things being meant to be, what do you say we leave that in God's hands?" With that, he was gone.

Alyssa stood staring at the empty doorway, joy filling her despite the heartbreak her decision to leave was causing her. Something good had come from her and Katie getting lost in the woods. Nathan had finally found his way back to the Lord.

With one final walk around the room to make certain she hadn't forgotten anything, she headed downstairs to say her goodbyes. The sight that greeted her in the parlor stopped her dead in her tracks. The small room was filled with people.

Heart pounding, she let her gaze do a slow sweep of the room, grateful that her vision had seemed to clear up from what it had been up-stairs. Carter and Logan stood at each end of the mantel, propped against it in a leisurely pose. There was no mistaking their tall, hulk-ing forms. And if she had to guess, she was sure they were both grinning. Doris and Myrna sat in the center of the room at the antique pedes-tal table, smiling. And to her left, Audra and the kids stood by the parlor window. Her gaze searched for the one face, with the exception of Nathan's, that she longed to see.

"I'm over here," a tiny voice called out, tug-ging at her heart.

She looked toward the deep burgundy Vic-torian love seat that sat in the far corner to see what could only be Katie seated there, wav-ing her hand excitedly. Dear, sweet, Katie. How would she ever be able to tell her goodbye?

"Hello, Katie," she said with a teary smile. She was going to miss seeing that adorable lit-tle face every day.

"I'm here, too."

She turned to see her best friend standing next to Doris and Myrna's beloved tea cart.

"Erica?" she gasped. "What are you doing here? I thought you had to work until four."

"Now what kind of best friend would I be if I stayed at work and missed this?" she said, sounding almost happy.

"Missed what?" Alyssa said in confusion.

"This," a deep voice said.

Her gaze shifted once again to find Nathan walking toward her. The look on his handsome face was one of determination. Reaching out, he took hold of her hand. "What are you doing?"

"Reckon you could say I'm putting my heart on the line," he replied, his tender gaze locking with hers.

"I don't understand," she said, searching his eyes.

"Maybe this will help," he said with a grin as he knelt in front of her.

Her soft gasp filled the parlor.

"Before you came into my life, I simply existed. Through your never-ending patience and your unyielding faith in God, you taught me how to truly live again." His thumb caressed the back of her hand. "How to love again."

"Nathan…" she began, her legs trembling beneath her.

"Hear me out, Alyssa," he implored. "A man only gets to do this once in his life. Twice if God sees fit to bless him with a second chance. You, Alyssa McCall, are my second chance."

Tears left wet trails down her cheeks, brought on by his beautiful words and the love she felt for the man kneeling before her.

"Daddy, you're making her cry," Katie said, sounding worried.

Laughing softly, she said, "They're happy tears, Katie. Very happy tears."

"I love you, Alyssa McCall," Nathan continued.

"Me, too!" Katie chimed in.

He chuckled, amending his words, "*We* love you. And we want you to be a part of our lives for as long as the good Lord sees fit. I know we've only been courting a short time, but you and I both know how fast life can change. I wanna spend whatever time I have left on this earth loving you. Working side by side. Laughing together. Alyssa McCall, will you do me the honor of agreeing to become my wife?"

"And my mommy!" Katie blurted out, the love seat creaking as she bounced up and down in delight.

"We don't have to get married right away. But I want us to keep moving forward," he said, looking up at her with undeniable love shining in his eyes. "When you're ready, say the word and we'll set the date."

"I…" She was so shocked, she could hardly speak.

He smiled warmly. A smile she would have the chance to see every day for the rest of her life if she chose to trust in the love he was offering her.

Looking down at Nathan, she returned his smile. "I would love nothing more than to be your wife."

"And my new mommy," Katie blurted out.

Nathan knew she would never try to take Isabel's place in Katie's life. But she would give his daughter what she needed. Another mother to care for her and help guide her into adulthood. "And," she added, her voice tight with emotion, "Katie's new mommy."

"Reckon my daddy was right," Nathan said, his tender gaze never leaving hers. "He told us boys there is always hope beyond the storm. And here you are, pushing away the dark clouds in my life and filling it with never-ending sunshine."

"Best get to sealing the deal," Carter hollered from across the room. "Before she up and changes her mind."

"She might even decide she'd rather marry me," Logan said with a teasing chuckle.

"Sorry, baby brother," Nathan shot back. "This girl is mine. You're gonna have to go find your own." Reaching into his shirt pocket, he withdrew a small blue ring box. Then he raised the lid, revealing a large solitaire flanked by two smaller diamonds."

"It's beautiful," Alyssa breathed, her heart pounding.

Taking the ring from its velvet nest, he slid it onto her finger and then stood, drawing her into his arms. "No, darlin', *you're* beautiful." Then he lowered his mouth to hers in a gentle, loving kiss.

"Alyssa was right," Katie squealed, pointing to the top of the entryway.

Everyone's gaze lifted to the sprig of dark green mistletoe tied in a cheery red ribbon that hung just above the newly engaged couple's heads.

"Kissing under the mistletoe makes two people wanna get married," Katie went on to explain in a way only a six-year-old could. Then she ran over to throw her arms around Nathan and Alyssa. "Now we'll get to be a real family."

"Yes, sweetie," Alyssa said, pressing a kiss to Katie's brow. "We most certainly will."

"Only I'm gonna have to change my Christmas list," Katie said with an exaggerated sigh.

"'Cause I already got what I was asking for—a mommy under the mistletoe."

Nathan chuckled. "What more could you want?"

Looking up at her daddy, she said, "I would like a dog just like Boone for Christmas…a really big picnic basket so we can go on lots of picnics together…and maybe a baby brother or sister."

With a chuckle, Nathan said, "It appears my daughter and I have the exact same Christmas list. With the exception of a brother or sister for Katie. That's gonna have to wait until next Christmas."

Laughter filled the room. And soon Alyssa found herself being embraced and congratulated, her heart overflowing with happiness. She had the love of a wonderful man, the precious gift of a child to love and someday soon she'd have a huge, loving family to call her very own.

# *Epilogue*

"Merry Christmas, darlin'," Nathan said as he came in from the kitchen to stand behind his beautiful fiancée, wrapping his arms around her waist as they stood admiring Katie's lovingly decorated Christmas tree.

She glanced up at him over her shoulder with a warm smile. "Merry Christmas to you, too. Were you able to get Katie's special surprise?"

"Took some doing," he said with a grin. Luckily for him, Carter had heard him pull up and had come out to help him round up the rambunctious pup he had been hiding in his brother's barn for the past two days. "Boone wasn't too happy about my taking his furry little friend away, but I told him they'd have plenty of time to play together in the future. Oh, and we're supposed to be at Carter's for Christmas dinner at four."

"My first Christmas dinner with your family," she said, her face alight with excitement.

"Soon to be your family, too," he reminded her.

Days before, with Alyssa and his daughter by his side, he had attended the church's annual Christmas program. One that had moved him both spiritually and emotionally. Then on Christmas Eve they had all gone together to the rec center for the dedication which had been a beautiful way to both cherish and finally let go of Isabel. He'd even made it through the Christmas festivities that followed without the darkness he used to feel any time he so much as thought about the holidays. The painful memories of his past had been replaced by new ones. Memories filled with family and friends, laughter and love, and so much more.

"The first of many," he added, his words a promise.

"Should we go wake Katie so you can give her the gift you got for her?"

"Not yet," he said with a tender smile. "First, I have a special surprise for you."

She turned in his arms, looking up at him with a teasing smile. "I'm getting a puppy, too?"

He chuckled softly. "Sorry to disappoint you, darlin', but your gift isn't nearly as fun." Leaning past her, he hooked a finger through one of the gift bags he'd set out around the tree the night before, lifting it from the assortment of prettily wrapped presents. "But," he said as he handed the glittery snowman gift bag to her, "I think you're gonna like it all the same. Why don't we have a seat on the sofa while you open it?"

"I already like it," she said as they walked over to the sofa and sat down. "I have a thing for snowmen."

"And handsome construction workers?" he added with a grin as he settled onto the sofa next to her.

Her smile widened. "*And* handsome construction workers. Especially one in particular."

He cupped her chin and tilted her face his way. "Well, I seem to have developed a thing for beautiful redheads."

A hint of color filled her cheeks. "My hair's not red. It's auburn."

"I stand corrected," he teased, lowering his mouth to hers in a sweet kiss. Then he pulled back and nodded toward the gift on her lap. "Best get to opening your present before Katie's special surprise figures out some way to escape the temporary wall I put up across the back porch steps."

Smiling, she reached into the bag and pulled out a tissue-wrapped bundle. Opening it carefully, she discovered there were several smaller tissue wrapped gifts inside. She peeled the paper away from the first and then held up the delicate glass ornament. "A bowling pin?"

"I know how much that ornament Doris and Myrna gave you means to you," he said. "I thought I'd add to your collection with some memories of our own."

Tears filled her eyes. "I love it."

He took the glass bowling pin from her, handing her another of the tissue-wrapped bundles.

She gasped when she opened it, holding the miniature picnic basket in the palm of her up-turned hand.

"This is for the inside picnic we shared," he told her. "And for all the picnics out under that big blue Texas sky we're gonna have in the years to come."

She sniffled, tears filling her eyes. "I can't wait to share those moments with you and Katie."

"One more," he said, taking the tiny basket and placing it atop the tissue it had been wrapped in.

"When did you have time to do all this?" she asked as she unrolled the wrapping from around the last piece.

"It's called online shopping with overnight shipping."

"Nathan," she gasped as she lifted from the tissue the ornament he'd made special for her.

The crystal teardrop ornament had come topped with mistletoe. He'd added a miniature hammer and paintbrush to it that he'd found in the dollhouse section of Rusty's toy store, attaching them to the mistletoe with the thinnest red ribbon he could find. "Reckon it was pretty enough without the fixings, but I thought the hammer and paintbrush made it more personal."

"It's perfect," she said, her words catching as she reached up to swipe a tear from her cheek. "I'll cherish it always." Reaching out for the gift she'd set on the end table when she'd arrived that morning, she handed it to him. "This is for you."

His smile widened as he took it. "A lump of coal?"

"Never," she replied. "Something I made special just for you."

His brow lifted as he eyed the gift with curiosity. "You made this, huh?" Peeling away the paper, he opened the top flaps of the box and pulled out a large, round, festively decorated Christmas tin. Then he lifted the lid, a wash of emotion coming over him. "You made me cookies."

"I have it on good authority that men have a thing for sweets," she explained with a smile. "And I decorated them all myself."

Inside the tin was at least two dozen iced sugar cookies. Each one had something differ-

ent written across them in red or green icing.
Love. Family. Forever. Yours. He lifted his gaze
to Alyssa. "I love you."

"I love you, too."

"Is it Christmas yet?" a tiny voice chirped
behind them.

They turned to find Katie standing in the living room entryway, attempting to suppress a
sleepy yawn.

"It sure is," Alyssa said gleefully. "And wait
until you see the special surprise your daddy
has for you."

Katie glanced toward the lit tree and the gifts
spread out beneath it, and her eyes widened.

Nathan helped Alyssa place her gifts back
into the gift bag and then stood. "Settle yourself onto the floor by the tree, Cupcake, while
I go get your special present."

Alyssa walked over to wait by the tree with
his daughter. Unable to keep the smile of happiness from his face, he went to get Katie's surprise, returning a couple of minutes later with
a very large picnic basket, a big red bow tied
around one of its handles.

"You got me a picnic basket!" his daughter
squealed in delight.

He set the basket onto the floor in front of her
and then stepped back to stand beside his fiancée, sliding an arm around her waist.

The basket wiggled, making Katie jump. Then a tiny whimper slid through its woven cracks. His daughter wasted no time pushing the handles down and whipping open the lid. A tiny beige head popped up and Katie exclaimed in delight. "It's a dog!"

"A puppy," Nathan corrected with a grin. "Which means we'll be doing a lot of cleaning up after her until she's housebroken."

She hefted the roly-poly little Lab pup from the basket and hugged it to her as it planted wet puppy kisses across her face. "I love her!"

"What are you gonna name her?" Alyssa asked as she knelt to pet the squirming ball of fur.

"I'm gonna name her Mistletoe," Katie announced as she attempted to dodge another onslaught of eager kisses.

"That's a pretty big name for such a little pup," Nathan said as he knelt next to his girls—all *three* of them.

"How about calling her Missy for short?" Alyssa suggested.

"Missy," Katie said, sounding it out. Then she lifted the pup, looking up into its round little face. "What do you think? Should I call you Missy?"

The pup barked excitedly. More to be let down to run wild than in appreciation of the name, Nathan thought with a grin, but it was all his daughter needed to settle on it. "Welcome to our family, Missy," Katie said, planting a kiss atop one of the pup's floppy tan ears. "This is the most special Christmas ever!"

Nathan looked to Alyssa, the woman who had rescued his heart, filling it with love, and his eyes misted over. God is good. "Yes, Cupcake," he said, his gaze meeting Alyssa's. "It surely is."

\* \* \* \* \*

*If you loved this story, pick up the first*
TEXAS SWEETHEARTS *book,*
*HER TEXAS HERO*
*from Love Inspired author Kat Brookes.*

*Available now from Love Inspired!*

*Find more great reads at*
*LoveInspired.com*

Dear Reader,

As my Texas Sweetheart series continues with *His Holiday Matchmaker*, you'll find a man still grieving the loss of his wife. Left to raise his young daughter alone, Nathan Cooper is struggling emotionally, as well as spiritually. The storm that took the lives of his wife and his parents has taken away his faith as well. Thankfully the Lord is patient and loving, and brings Alyssa McCall into his and his daughter's lives. This is when the true healing begins.

Last year, days before Christmas, I lost my beloved mother-in-law to an unfortunate accident. I understand on a more personal level now how Nathan could have questioned his losses. I have gone through so many emotions during the past several months, but, unlike Nathan, I have been able to cling to my faith. Loss happens, so we all need to thankful for the precious time we are given to spend with those we care about.

Be sure to watch for the final book in the Texas Sweetheart series, which will be out in 2017.

I love to hear from my readers. You can contact me via my email: katbrookes@comcast.

net or through Facebook. News and book release information can be found on my website—
www.katbrookes.com

*Kat Brookes*

# LARGER-PRINT BOOKS!

## GET 2 FREE
## LARGER-PRINT NOVELS
## PLUS 2 FREE
## MYSTERY GIFTS

*Love Inspired®*

# SUSPENSE
### RIVETING INSPIRATIONAL ROMANCE

## Larger-print novels are now available...

---

# REQUEST YOUR FREE BOOKS!
## 2 FREE WHOLESOME ROMANCE NOVELS IN LARGER PRINT
## PLUS 2 FREE MYSTERY GIFTS

✿✿✿✿✿✿✿✿✿✿✿✿✿✿✿✿✿✿✿✿

# HEARTWARMING™

❀❀❀❀❀❀❀❀❀❀❀❀❀❀❀❀❀❀❀❀

*Wholesome, tender romances*

**YES!** Please send me 2 FREE Harlequin® Heartwarming Larger-Print novels and my 2 FREE mystery gifts (gifts worth about $10). After receiving them, if I don't wish to receive any more books, I can return the shipping statement marked "cancel." If I don't cancel, I will receive 4 brand-new larger-print novels every month and be billed just $5.24 per book in the U.S. or $5.99 per book in Canada. That's a savings of at least 19% off the cover price. It's quite a bargain! Shipping and handling is just 50¢ per book in the U.S. and 75¢ per book in Canada.* I understand that accepting the 2 free books and gifts places me under no obligation to buy anything. I can always return a shipment and cancel at any time. Even if I never buy another book, the two free books and gifts are mine to keep forever.

161/361 IDN GHX2

| Name | (PLEASE PRINT) | |
| --- | --- | --- |
| Address | | Apt. # |
| City | State/Prov. | Zip/Postal Code |

Signature (if under 18, a parent or guardian must sign)

Mail to the **Reader Service:**
**IN U.S.A.:** P.O. Box 1867, Buffalo, NY 14240-1867
**IN CANADA:** P.O. Box 609, Fort Erie, Ontario L2A 5X3

\* Terms and prices subject to change without notice. Prices do not include applicable taxes. Sales tax applicable in N.Y. Canadian residents will be charged applicable taxes. Offer not valid in Quebec. This offer is limited to one order per household. Not valid for current subscribers to Harlequin Heartwarming larger-print books. All orders subject to credit approval. Credit or debit balances in a customer's account(s) may be offset by any other outstanding balance owed by or to the customer. Please allow 4 to 6 weeks for delivery. Offer available while quantities last.

**Your Privacy**—The Reader Service is committed to protecting your privacy. Our Privacy Policy is available online at www.ReaderService.com or upon request from the Reader Service.

We make a portion of our mailing list available to reputable third parties that offer products we believe may interest you. If you prefer that we not exchange your name with third parties, or if you wish to clarify or modify your communication preferences, please visit us at www.ReaderService.com/consumerchoice or write to us at Reader Service Preference Service, P.O. Box 9062, Buffalo, NY 14240-9062. Include your complete name and address.

HW15

# WESTERN (WP) PROMISES

**YES!** Please send me **The Western Promises Collection** in Larger Print. This collection begins with 3 FREE books and 2 FREE gifts (gifts valued at approx. $14.00 retail) in the first shipment, along with the other first 4 books from the collection! If I do not cancel, I will receive 8 monthly shipments until I have the entire 51-book Western Promises collection. I will receive 2 or 3 FREE books in each shipment and I will pay just $4.99 US/ $5.89 CDN for each of the other four books in each shipment, plus $2.99 for shipping and handling per shipment. *If I decide to keep the entire collection, I'll have paid for only 32 books, because 19 books are FREE! I understand that accepting the 3 free books and gifts places me under no obligation to buy anything. I can always return a shipment and cancel at any time. My free books and gifts are mine to keep no matter what I decide.

272 HCN 3070 472 HCN 3070

| | |
|---|---|
| Name | (PLEASE PRINT) |
| Address | Apt. # |
| City | State/Prov.     Zip/Postal Code |

Signature (if under 18, a parent or guardian must sign)

### Mail to the **Reader Service**:

**IN U.S.A.:** P.O. Box 1867, Buffalo, NY 14240-1867
**IN CANADA:** P.O. Box 609, Fort Erie, Ontario L2A 5X3

WPBPA16R